KALOS
REGION HANDBOOK

STATS AND FACTS ON OVER 450 POKÉMON!

ISBN 978-0-545-64602-4

10 9 8 7 6 5 4 3   14 15 16 17 18 19/0
Printed in the U.S.A.   40
First printing, August 2014

CONTENTS

Meet the Kalos Pokémon

Welcome to the Kalos region! Here you'll encounter many new Pokémon—plus learn about exciting new skills some of your favorite Pokémon have developed.

The key to success with Pokémon is staying informed. Information about each Pokémon's type, height, and weight can make all the difference in raising, battling, and evolving your Pokémon

In this book, you'll get all the stats and facts you need about the Pokémon of Kalos. You'll find out how each Pokémon evolves, which Moves it uses, and learn which Pokémon can evolve into Mega-Evolved Pokémon during battle.

So get ready, Trainers: With this guide, you'll be ready to master almost any Pokémon challenge!

How to Use This Book

Here are the basics you'll discover about each Pokémon:

NAME

CATEGORY

HOW TO SAY IT

When it comes to Pokémon pronunciation, it's easy to get tongue-tied! There are many Pokémon with unusual names, so we'll help you sound them out. Soon you'll be saying Pokémon names so perfectly, you'll sound like a professor!

HEIGHT AND WEIGHT

How does each Pokémon measure up? Find out by checking its height and weight stats. And remember, good things come in all shapes and sizes. It's up to every Trainer to work with his or her Pokémon and play up its size.

POSSIBLE MOVES

Every Pokémon has its own unique combination of Moves. Before you hit the battlefield, we'll tell you all about each Pokémon's awesome attacks. And don't forget, with a good Trainer, they can always learn more!

DESCRIPTION

Knowledge is power! Pokémon Trainers have to know their stuff. Find out everything you need to know about your Pokémon here.

EVOLUTION

If your Pokémon has an evolved form or pre-evolved form, we'll show you its place in the chain and how it evolves.

MEGA EVOLUTION

In Kalos, certain key Pokémon have an all-new skill—during battle, they can Mega Evolve. They can tap into strength far greater than anything they've ever experienced. They can change height, weight, and even type. You'll get the new stats in this book.

TYPE

Each Pokémon has a type, and some even have two! (Pokémon with two types are called dual-type Pokémon.) Every type of Pokémon comes with its advantages and disadvantages. We'll break them all down for you here.

Curious about what Pokémon types you can spot in Kalos? Find out about all eighteen types on the next page . . .

Guide to Pokémon Types

A Pokémon's type can tell you a lot about it—from where to find it in the wild to the Moves it'll be able to use on the battlefield. Type is the key to unlocking a Pokémon's power.

A clever Trainer should always consider type when picking a Pokémon for a match, because type shows a Pokémon's strengths and weaknesses. For example, a Fire type may melt an Ice type, but against a Water type, it might find it's the one in hot water. And while a Water type usually has the upper hand in battle with a Fire type, a Water-type Move would act like a sprinkler on a Grass-type Pokémon. But when that same Grass type is battling a Fire type, it just might get scorched.

Keep in mind that Moves can be mightier based on the location of the battle. Rock-type Pokémon rock at mountainside battles, Electric types get charged up near power plants, and Ground types like to get down and dirty right in the dirt. And if a Pokémon has two types—that is, if it's a dual type—well, then it's double trouble!

Here are the eighteen different Pokémon types:

FIRE

GRASS

WATER

NORMAL

ELECTRIC

BUG

GHOST

FLYING

FIGHTING

PSYCHIC

STEEL

ROCK

GROUND

ICE

POISON

DARK

DRAGON

FAIRY

Welcome to the Kalos Central Subregion!

Welcome to the heartland of Kalos! The Central subregion has many fertile farms, gardens, and parks. It's also known for its fast-flowing rivers.

The Central Subregion is famous for its amazing Flying-type, Bug-type, and Grass-type Pokémon, including Gogoat, Charizard, and the rainbow-colored Vivillon—plus partner Pokémon Chespin, Fennekin, and Froakie. Discover how many Central Region Pokémon you already know—and meet some new ones!

TYPE:
PSYCHIC

How to say it: AH-bra

Height: 2' 11"
Weight: 43.0 lbs.

Possible Moves: Teleport

Even when it's asleep—which is most of the time—Abra can sense an attack coming and teleport away.

Abra   Kadabra   Alakazam   Mega Alakazam

AEGISLASH
Royal Sword Pokémon

Blade Forme

TYPE:
STEEL-
GHOST

How to say it: EE-jih-SLASH

Height: 5' 07"
Weight: 116.8 lbs.

Possible Moves: Fury Cutter, Pursuit, Autotomize, Shadow Sneak, Slash, Iron Defense, Night Slash, Power Trick, Iron Head, Head Smash, Swords Dance, Aerial Ace, King's Shield, Sacred Sword

Aegislash has long been seen as a symbol of royalty. In olden days, these Pokémon often accompanied the king.

Shield Forme

Honedge → Doublade → Aegislash

ALAKAZAM
Psi Pokémon

How to say it: AH-la-kuh-ZAM

Height: 4' 11"
Weight: 105.8 lbs.

Possible Moves: Teleport, Kinesis, Confusion, Disable, Miracle Eye, Ally Switch, Psybeam, Reflect, Telekinesis, Recover, Psycho Cut, Calm Mind, Psychic, Future Sight, Trick

With its dizzying intellect, Alakazam remembers everything that happens to it. A supercomputer is no match for its incredible brain.

MEGA ALAKAZAM
Psi Pokémon

Height: 3' 11"
Weight: 105.8 lbs.

TYPE:
PSYCHIC

Abra → Kadabra → Alakazam → Mega Alakazam

AROMATISSE
Fragrance Pokémon

TYPE: FAIRY

How to say it: Uh-ROME-uh-teece

Height: 2' 07"   **Weight:** 34.2 lbs.

Possible Moves: Aromatic Mist, Heal Pulse, Sweet Scent, Fairy Wind, Sweet Kiss, Odor Sleuth, Echoed Voice, Calm Mind, Draining Kiss, Aromatherapy, Attract, Moonblast, Charm, Flail, Misty Terrain, Skill Swap, Psychic, Disarming Voice, Reflect, Psych Up

Aromatisse uses its powerful scent as a weapon in battle. It can overpower an opponent with a strategic stench.

Spritzee   Aromatisse

AUDINO
Hearing Pokémon

TYPE: NORMAL

How to say it: AW-dih-noh

Height: 3' 07"   **Weight:** 68.3 lbs.

Possible Moves: Last Resort, Play Nice, Pound, Growl, Helping Hand, Refresh, Double Slap, Attract, Secret Power, Entrainment, Take Down, Heal Pulse, After You, Simple Beam, Double-Edge

With the sensitive feelers on their ears, Audino can listen to people's heartbeats to pick up on their current state. Egg-hatching can be predicted as well.

Does not evolve

How to say it: AKS-yoo

Height: 2' 00"   **Weight:** 39.7 lbs.

Possible Moves: Scratch, Leer, Assurance, Dragon Rage, Dual Chop, Scary Face, Slash, False Swipe, Dragon Claw, Dragon Dance, Taunt, Dragon Pulse, Swords Dance, Guillotine, Outrage, Giga Impact

If one of Axew's tusks breaks off, it quickly regrows, even stronger and sharper than before. It uses its tusks to crush berries and mark territory.

TYPE: DRAGON

Axew → Fraxure → Haxorus

AZUMARILL
Aqua Rabbit Pokémon

How to say it: ah-ZU-mare-rill

Height: 2' 07"
Weight: 62.8 lbs.

TYPE:
WATER-
FAIRY

Possible Moves: Tackle, Water Gun, Tail Whip, Water Sport, Bubble, Defense Curl, Rollout, Bubble Beam, Helping Hand, Aqua Tail, Double-Edge, Aqua Ring, Rain Dance, Superpower, Hydro Pump, Play Rough

With its long ears, Azumarill can sense when a living thing is moving at the bottom of the river. Its bubble-patterned belly serves as camouflage when it swims.

Azurill → Marill → Azumarill

AZURILL
Polka Dot Pokémon

TYPE:
NORMAL-
FAIRY

How to say it: uh-ZOO-rill

Height: 0' 08"   **Weight:** 4.4 lbs.

Possible Moves: Splash, Water Gun, Tail Whip, Water Sport, Bubble, Charm, Bubble Beam, Helping Hand, Slam, Bounce

When fighting off a large attacker, Azurill swings its bulbous tail around like a weight. It can also bounce on its tail to get around on land.

Azurill → Marill → Azumarill

BEEDRILL
Poison Bee Pokémon

How to say it: BEE-dril

Height: 3' 03" **Weight:** 65.0 lbs.

Possible Moves: Fury Attack, Focus Energy, Twineedle, Rage, Pursuit, Toxic Spikes, Pin Missile, Agility, Assurance, Poison Jab, Endeavor, Fell Stinger

Beedrill wields its three stingers viciously, jabbing at an opponent with their poisoned tips. Sometimes a group of Beedrill will swarm a single enemy.

Weedle ➡ Kakuna ➡ Beedrill

TYPE:
BUG-POISON

BELLOSSOM
Flower Pokémon

How to say it: bell-LAHS-um

Height: 1' 04" **Weight:** 12.8 lbs.

Possible Moves: Leaf Storm, Leaf Blade, Mega Drain, Sweet Scent, Stun Spore, Sunny Day, Magical Leaf, Petal Blizzard

When Bellossom come together to dance after a heavy rain, some say they're performing a ritual to draw the sun back into the sky.

TYPE:
GRASS

Vileplume

Oddish   Gloom

Bellossom

BIBAREL
Beaver Pokémon

TYPE:
NORMAL-
WATER

How to say it: bee-BER-rel

Height: 3' 03"   **Weight:** 69.4 lbs.

Possible Moves: Rototiller, Tackle, Growl, Defense Curl, Rollout, Water Gun, Headbutt, Hyper Fang, Yawn, Amnesia, Take Down, Super Fang, Superpower, Curse

With their large, sharp teeth, Bibarel busily cut up trees to build nests. Sometimes these nests block small streams and divert the flow of the water.

Bidoof   Bibarel

BIDOOF
Plump Mouse Pokémon

TYPE:
NORMAL

How to say it: BEE-doof

Height: 1' 08"   **Weight:** 44.1 lbs.

Possible Moves: Tackle, Growl, Defense Curl, Rollout, Headbutt, Hyper Fang, Yawn, Amnesia, Take Down, Super Fang, Superpower, Curse

Bidoof live beside the water, where they gnaw on rock or wood to keep their front teeth worn down. They have a steady nature and are not easily upset.

Bidoof   Bibarel

BLASTOISE
Shellfish Pokémon

How to say it: BLAS-toyce

Height: 5' 03"   **Weight:** 188.5 lbs.

Possible Moves: Flash Cannon, Tackle, Tail Whip, Water Gun, Withdraw, Bubble, Bite, Rapid Spin, Protect, Water Pulse, Aqua Tail, Skull Bash, Iron Defense, Rain Dance, Hydro Pump

The rocket cannons on Blastoise's shell shoot water jets powerful enough to punch through thick steel.

TYPE:
WATER

MEGA BLASTOISE
Shellfish Pokémon

Height: 5' 03"
Weight: 222.9 lbs.

TYPE:
WATER

Squirtle → Wartortle → Blastoise → Mega Blastoise

BRAIXEN
Fox Pokémon

TYPE:
FIRE

How to say it: BRAKE-sen

Height: 3' 03"   **Weight:** 32.0 lbs.

Possible Moves: Scratch, Tail Whip, Ember, Howl, Flame Charge, Psybeam, Fire Spin, Lucky Chant, Light Screen, Psyshock, Flamethrower, Will-O-Wisp, Psychic, Sunny Day, Magic Room, Fire Blast

When Braixen pulls the twig out of its tail, the friction from its fur sets the wood on fire. It can use this flaming twig as a tool or a weapon.

Fennekin   Braixen   Delphox

BUDEW
Bud Pokémon

TYPE:
GRASS-POISON

How to say it: buh-DOO

Height: 0' 08"   **Weight:** 2.6 lbs.

Possible Moves: Absorb, Growth, Water Sport, Stun Spore, Mega Drain, Worry Seed

When the weather turns cold, Budew's bud is tightly closed. In the springtime, it opens up again and gives off its pollen.

Budew   Roselia   Roserade

BULBASAUR
Seed Pokémon

How to say it: BUL-ba-sore

Height: 2' 04"   **Weight:** 15.2 lbs.

Possible Moves: Tackle, Growl, Leech Seed, Vine Whip, Poison Powder, Sleep Powder, Take Down, Razor Leaf, Sweet Scent, Growth, Double-Edge, Worry Seed, Synthesis, Seed Bomb

Once it hatches, a Bulbasaur uses the seed on its back for the nutrients it needs in order to grow.

TYPE: GRASS-POISON

Bulbasaur   Ivysaur   Venusaur   Mega Venusaur

BUNNELBY
Digging Pokémon

How to say it: BUN-ell-bee

Height: 1' 04"   **Weight:** 11.0 lbs.

Possible Moves: Tackle, Agility, Leer, Quick Attack, Double Slap, Mud-Slap, Take Down, Mud Shot, Double Kick, Odor Sleuth, Flail, Dig, Bounce, Super Fang, Facade, Earthquake

Bunnelby can use its ears like shovels to dig holes in the ground. Eventually, its ears become strong enough to cut through thick tree roots while it digs.

TYPE: NORMAL

Bunnelby   Diggersby

BURMY (GRASS CLOAK)
Bagworm Pokémon

TYPE:
BUG

How to say it: BURR-mee

Height: 0' 08"   **Weight:** 7.5 lbs.

Possible Moves: Protect, Tackle, Bug Bite, Hidden Power

Burmy can camouflage itself by burying itself in leaves and twigs. If it's uncovered in battle, it quickly covers itself back up.

Wormadam
Female Form

Mothim
Male Form

Burmy

BURMY (SANDY CLOAK)
Bagworm Pokémon

TYPE:
BUG

How to say it: BURR-mee

Height: 0' 08"   **Weight:** 7.5 lbs.

Possible Moves: Protect, Tackle, Bug Bite, Hidden Power

Did you know that each Burmy covers up with the objects around it? This Burmy uses rocks and sand for protection.

Wormadam
Female Form

Mothim
Male Form

Burmy

BURMY (TRASH CLOAK)
Bagworm Pokémon

How to say it: BURR-mee

Height: 0' 08"   **Weight:** 7.5 lbs.

Possible Moves: Protect, Tackle, Bug Bite, Hidden Power

If you're looking for Burmy with a Trash Cloak, try poking around inside a few buildings. You might get lucky!

TYPE:
BUG

Burmy → Wormadam Female Form

Burmy → Mothim Male Form

BUTTERFREE
Butterfly Pokémon

TYPE:
BUG-
FLYING

How to say it: BUT-er-free

Height: 3' 07"   **Weight:** 70.5 lbs.

Possible Moves: Confusion, Poison Powder, Stun Spore, Sleep Powder, Gust, Supersonic, Whirlwind, Psybeam, Silver Wind, Tailwind, Rage Powder, Safeguard, Captivate, Bug Buzz, Quiver Dance

The dust on its wings repels water, so Butterfree has no problems flying in the rain. It seeks out flowers for their tasty nectar.

Caterpie → Metapod → Butterfree

CARVANHA
Savage Pokémon

TYPE:
WATER-
DARK

How to say it: car-VAH-na

Height: 2' 07"   **Weight:** 45.9 lbs.

Possible Moves: Leer, Bite, Rage, Focus Energy, Scary Face, Ice Fang, Screech, Swagger, Assurance, Crunch, Aqua Jet, Agility, Take Down

Carvanha swarm around any boat that enters their territory, ripping at the boats' hulls in furious attack. The rivers where they live are surrounded by dense jungle.

Carvanha   Sharpedo

CATERPIE
Worm Pokémon

TYPE:
BUG

How to say it: CAT-ur-pee

Height: 1' 00"   **Weight:** 6.4 lbs.

Possible Moves: Tackle, String Shot, Bug Bite

Caterpie's red antennae can produce a terrible smell to repel attackers. Its suction-cup feet stick to any surface, so it can climb high into the trees for food.

Caterpie   Metapod   Butterfree

TYPE:
FIRE-
FLYING

CHARIZARD
Flame Pokémon

How to say it: CHAR-iz-ard

Height: 5' 07"   **Weight:** 199.5 lbs.

Possible Moves: Flare Blitz, Heat Wave, Dragon Claw, Shadow Claw, Air Slash, Scratch, Growl, Ember, Smokescreen, Dragon Rage, Scary Face, Fire Fang, Flame Burst, Wing Attack, Slash, Flamethrower, Fire Spin, Inferno

It's said that the more hard battles a Charizard has fought, the hotter its fire will burn.

MEGA CHARIZARD X
Flame Pokémon

Height: 5' 07"
Weight: 243.6 lbs.

TYPE:
FIRE-
DRAGON

MEGA CHARIZARD Y
Flame Pokémon

Height: 5' 07"
Weight: 221.6 lbs.

TYPE:
FIRE-
FLYING

Charmander → **Charmeleon** → **Charizard**

Mega Charizard X

Mega Charizard Y

CHARMANDER

Lizard Pokémon

TYPE: FIRE

How to say it: CHAR-man-der

Height: 2' 00"　**Weight:** 18.7 lbs.

Possible Moves: Scratch, Growl, Ember, Smokescreen, Dragon Rage, Scary Face, Fire Fang, Flame Burst, Slash, Flamethrower, Fire Spin, Inferno

The flame on the tip of a Charmander's tail is a key to its current state. A healthy Charmander has an intense tail flame.

 **Mega Charizard X**

 **Mega Charizard Y**

Charmander　Charmeleon　Charizard

CHARMELEON

Flame Pokémon

TYPE: FIRE

How to say it: char-MEE-lee-un

Height: 3' 07"　**Weight:** 41.9 lbs.

Possible Moves: Scratch, Growl, Ember, Smokescreen, Dragon Rage, Scary Face, Fire Fang, Flame Burst, Slash, Flamethrower, Fire Spin, Inferno

When night falls in the rocky mountains where Charmeleon live, the fires on their tails can be seen glowing like stars.

 Mega Charizard X

 Mega Charizard Y

Charmander　Charmeleon　Charizard

CHESNAUGHT

Spiny Armor Pokémon

TYPE:
GRASS-
FIGHTING

How to say it: CHESS-nawt

Height: 5' 03"   **Weight:** 198.4 lbs.

Possible Moves: Feint, Hammer Arm, Belly Drum, Tackle, Growl, Vine Whip, Rollout, Bite, Leech Seed, Pin Missile, Needle Arm, Take Down, Seed Bomb, Spiky Shield, Mud Shot, Bulk Up, Body Slam, Pain Split, Wood Hammer, Giga Impact

When its friends are in trouble, Chesnaught uses its own body as a shield. Its shell is tough enough to protect it from a powerful explosion.

Chespin   Quilladin   Chesnaught

CHESPIN

Spiny Nut Pokémon

How to say it: CHESS-pin

Height: 1' 04"   **Weight:** 19.8 lbs.

Possible Moves: Tackle, Growl, Vine Whip, Rollout, Bite, Leech Seed, Pin Missile, Take Down, Seed Bomb, Mud Shot, Bulk Up, Body Slam, Pain Split, Wood Hammer

When Chespin flexes its soft quills, they become tough spikes with sharp, piercing points. It relies on its nutlike shell for protection in battle.

TYPE:
GRASS

Chespin   Quilladin   Chesnaught

COMBEE
Tiny Bee Pokémon

TYPE:
BUG-
FLYING

How to say it: COMB-bee

Height: 1' 00"   **Weight:** 12.1 lbs.

Possible Moves: Sweet Scent, Gust, Bug Bite, Bug Buzz

Combee are always in search of honey, which they bring to their Vespiquen leader. They cluster together to sleep in a formation that resembles a hive.

Combee   Vespiquen

CORPHISH
Ruffian Pokémon

How to say it: COR-fish

Height: 2' 00"   **Weight:** 25.4 lbs.

Possible Moves: Bubble, Harden, Vice Grip, Leer, Bubble Beam, Protect, Knock Off, Taunt, Night Slash, Crabhammer, Swords Dance, Crunch, Guillotine

The hardy Corphish can thrive even in very polluted rivers. Once its pincers catch hold of something, it never lets go.

TYPE:
WATER

Corphish   Crawdaunt

CRAWDAUNT

Rogue Pokémon

TYPE:
WATER-
DARK

How to say it: CRAW-daunt

Height: 3' 07"   **Weight:** 72.3 lbs.

Possible Moves: Guillotine, Bubble, Harden, Vice Grip, Leer, Bubble Beam, Protect, Knock Off, Swift, Taunt, Night Slash, Crabhammer, Swords Dance, Crunch

Feisty and territorial, Crawdaunt uses its pincers to fling any intruders out of the pond where it lives.

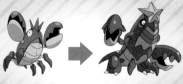

Corphish   Crawdaunt

CROAGUNK
Toxic Mouth Pokémon

How to say it: CROW-gunk

Height: 2' 04"   **Weight:** 50.7 lbs.

Possible Moves: Astonish, Mud-Slap, Poison Sting, Taunt, Pursuit, Feint Attack, Revenge, Swagger, Mud Bomb, Sucker Punch, Venoshock, Nasty Plot, Poison Jab, Sludge Bomb, Belch, Flatter

Croagunk produces its distinctive croaking sound by inflating the poison sacs in its cheeks. The sound often startles an opponent so it can get in a poisonous jab.

TYPE: POISON-FIGHTING

Croagunk   Toxicroak

CROBAT
Bat Pokémon

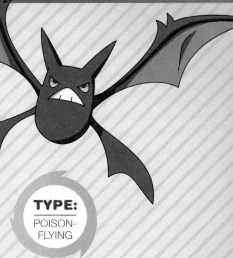

How to say it: CROW-bat

Height: 5' 11"   **Weight:** 165.3 lbs.

Possible Moves: Cross Poison, Screech, Leech Life, Supersonic, Astonish, Bite, Wing Attack, Confuse Ray, Swift, Air Cutter, Acrobatics, Mean Look, Poison Fang, Haze, Air Slash

Hunting in darkness, Crobat can maintain absolute silence. Its four wings let it fly quickly, without sound.

TYPE: POISON-FLYING

Zubat   Golbat   Crobat

How to say it: dell-CAT-tee

Height: 3' 07"   **Weight:** 71.9 lbs.

Possible Moves: Fake Out, Attract, Sing, Double Slap

Because of its beautiful fur, stylish Trainers favor Delcatty. It looks for a clean and comfortable place where it can settle in to groom itself.

TYPE:
NORMAL

Skitty ➡ **Delcatty**

DELPHOX
Fox Pokémon

How to say it: DELL-fox

Height: 4' 11"   **Weight:** 86.0 lbs.

Possible Moves: Future Sight, Role Play, Switcheroo, Shadow Ball, Scratch, Tail Whip, Ember, Howl, Flame Charge, Psybeam, Fire Spin, Lucky Chant, Light Screen, Psyshock, Mystical Fire, Flamethrower, Will-O-Wisp, Psychic, Sunny Day, Magic Room, Fire Blast

The mystical Delphox uses a flaming branch as a focus for its psychic visions. When it gazes into the fire, it can see the future.

TYPE:
FIRE-
PSYCHIC

Fennekin ➡ **Braixen** ➡ **Delphox**

DIGGERSBY
Digging Pokémon

How to say it: DIH-gurz-bee

Height: 3' 03"   **Weight:** 93.5 lbs.

Possible Moves: Hammer Arm, Rototiller, Bulldoze, Swords Dance, Tackle, Agility, Leer, Quick Attack, Mud-Slap, Take Down, Mud Shot, Double Kick, Odor Sleuth, Flail, Dig, Bounce, Super Fang, Facade, Earthquake

Diggersby can use their ears like excavators to move heavy boulders. Construction workers like having them around.

TYPE:
NORMAL-
GROUND

Bunnelby   Diggersby

DODRIO
Triple Bird Pokémon

TYPE:
NORMAL-
FLYING

How to say it: doe-DREE-oh

Height: 5' 11"   **Weight:** 187.8 lbs.

Possible Moves: Pluck, Peck, Growl, Quick Attack, Rage, Fury Attack, Pursuit, Uproar, Acupressure, Tri Attack, Agility, Drill Peck, Endeavor, Thrash

With its swift beaks, Dodrio can deliver relentless pecking attacks. Its three heads display different emotions.

Doduo   Dodrio

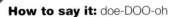

DODUO
Twin Bird Pokémon

How to say it: doe-DOO-oh

Height: 4' 07"   **Weight:** 86.4 lbs.

Possible Moves: Peck, Growl, Quick Attack, Rage, Fury Attack, Pursuit, Uproar, Acupressure, Double Hit, Agility, Drill Peck, Endeavor, Thrash

The two-headed Doduo could keep pace with a car on the highway. Its brains seem to use telepathy to communicate.

TYPE:
NORMAL-
FLYING

Doduo   Dodrio

DOUBLADE
Sword Pokémon

How to say it: DUH-blade

Height: 2' 07"   **Weight:** 9.9 lbs.

Possible Moves: Tackle, Swords Dance, Fury Cutter, Metal Sound, Pursuit, Autotomize, Shadow Sneak, Aerial Ace, Retaliate, Slash, Iron Defense, Night Slash, Power Trick, Iron Head, Sacred Sword

The two swords that make up Doublade's body fight together in intricate slashing patterns that bewilder even accomplished swordsmen.

TYPE:
STEEL-
GHOST

Honedge   Doublade   Aegislash

DUCKLETT
Water Bird Pokémon

TYPE:
WATER-FLYING

How to say it: DUK-lit

Height: 1' 08"   **Weight:** 12.1 lbs.

Possible Moves: Water Gun, Water Sport, Defog, Wing Attack, Water Pulse, Aerial Ace, Bubble Beam, Feather Dance, Aqua Ring, Air Slash, Roost, Rain Dance, Tailwind, Brave Bird, Hurricane

Skilled swimmers, Ducklett dive underwater in search of delicious peat moss. When enemies approach, they kick up water with their wings to cover their retreat.

Ducklett   Swanna

DUNSPARCE
Land Snake Pokémon

TYPE:
NORMAL

How to say it: DUN-sparce

Height: 4' 11"   **Weight:** 30.9 lbs.

Possible Moves: Rage, Defense Curl, Rollout, Spite, Pursuit, Screech, Yawn, Ancient Power, Take Down, Roost, Glare, Dig, Double-Edge, Coil, Endure, Drill Run, Endeavor, Flail

To escape from an enemy, Dunsparce digs frantically with its tail to burrow backward into the ground. Its subterranean nest resembles a maze.

Does not evolve

How to say it: ESS-purr

Height: 1' 00"   **Weight:** 7.7 lbs.

Possible Moves: Scratch, Leer, Covet, Confusion, Light Screen, Psybeam, Fake Out, Disarming Voice, Psyshock

Espurr emits powerful psychic energy from organs in its ears. It has to fold its ears down to keep the power contained.

TYPE: PSYCHIC

Espurr   Meowstic

EXPLOUD
Loud Noise Pokémon

TYPE: NORMAL

How to say it: ecks-PLOWD

Height: 4' 11"   **Weight:** 185.2 lbs.

Possible Moves: Ice Fang, Fire Fang, Thunder Fang, Pound, Uproar, Astonish, Howl, Bite, Supersonic, Stomp, Screech, Crunch, Roar, Synchronoise, Rest, Sleep Talk, Hyper Voice, Hyper Beam, Boomburst

The ports all over Exploud's body create different sounds when air blows through them. Exploud's battle cry shakes the ground around it and can be heard miles away.

Whismur   Loudred   Exploud

FARFETCH'D
Wild Duck Pokémon

TYPE:
NORMAL-
FLYING

How to say it: FAR-fetched

Height: 2' 07"
Weight: 33.1 lbs.

Possible Moves: Brave Bird, Poison Jab, Peck, Sand Attack, Leer, Fury Cutter, Fury Attack, Aerial Ace, Knock Off, Slash, Air Cutter, Swords Dance, Agility, Night Slash, Acrobatics, Feint, False Swipe, Air Slash

Farfetch'd always carries its trusty plant stalk. It can brandish the stalk like a weapon or use it to build a nest.

Does not evolve

FENNEKIN
Fox Pokémon

TYPE:
FIRE

How to say it: FEN-ik-in

Height: 1' 04"   **Weight:** 20.7 lbs.

Possible Moves: Scratch, Tail Whip, Ember, Howl, Flame Charge, Psybeam, Fire Spin, Lucky Chant, Light Screen, Psyshock, Flamethrower, Will-O-Wisp, Psychic, Sunny Day, Magic Room, Fire Blast

Searing heat radiates from Fennekin's large ears to keep opponents at a distance. It often snacks on twigs to gain energy.

Fennekin   Braixen   Delphox

FLABÉBÉ
Single Bloom Pokémon

How to say it: flah-BAY-BAY

Height: 0' 04"   **Weight:** 0.2 lbs.

Possible Moves: Tackle, Vine Whip, Fairy Wind, Lucky Chant, Razor Leaf, Wish, Magical Leaf, Grassy Terrain, Petal Blizzard, Aromatherapy, Misty Terrain, Moonblast, Petal Dance, Solar Beam

Each Flabébé has a special connection with the flower it holds. They take care of their flowers and use them as an energy source.

TYPE:
FAIRY

Flabébé   Floette   Florges

FLETCHINDER
Ember Pokémon

How to say it: FLETCH-in-der

Height: 2' 04"
Weight: 35.3 lbs.

Possible Moves: Tackle, Growl, Quick Attack, Peck, Agility, Flail, Ember, Roost, Razor Wind, Natural Gift, Flame Charge, Acrobatics, Me First, Tailwind, Steel Wing

As the flame sac on Fletchinder's belly slowly heats up, it flies faster and faster. It produces embers from its beak.

TYPE:
FIRE-
FLYING

Fletchling Fletchinder Talonflame

FLETCHLING
Tiny Robin Pokémon

TYPE: NORMAL-FLYING

How to say it: FLETCH-ling

Height: 1' 00"   **Weight:** 3.7 lbs.

Possible Moves: Tackle, Growl, Quick Attack, Peck, Agility, Flail, Roost, Razor Wind, Natural Gift, Flame Charge, Acrobatics, Me First, Tailwind, Steel Wing

To communicate, flocks of Fletchling sing to one another in beautiful voices. If an intruder threatens their territory, they will defend it fiercely.

Fletchling Fletchinder Talonflame

FLOETTE
Single Bloom Pokémon

TYPE: FAIRY

How to say it: floh-ET

Height: 0' 08"   **Weight:** 2.0 lbs.

Possible Moves: Tackle, Vine Whip, Fairy Wind, Lucky Chant, Razor Leaf, Wish, Magical Leaf, Grassy Terrain, Petal Blizzard, Aromatherapy, Misty Terrain, Moonblast, Petal Dance, Solar Beam

Floette keeps watch over flower beds and will rescue a flower if it starts to droop. It dances to celebrate the spring bloom.

Flabébé   Floette   Florges

FLORGES
Garden Pokémon

How to say it: FLORE-jess

Height: 3' 07"
Weight: 22.0 lbs.

Possible Moves: Disarming Voice, Lucky Chant, Wish, Magical Leaf, Flower Shield, Grass Knot, Grassy Terrain, Petal Blizzard, Misty Terrain, Moonblast, Petal Dance, Aromatherapy

TYPE:
FAIRY

Long ago, Florges were a welcome sight on castle grounds, where they would create elaborate flower gardens.

Flabébé → Floette → Florges

FRAXURE
Axe Jaw Pokémon

How to say it: FRAK-shur

Height: 3' 03"
Weight: 79.4 lbs.

Possible Moves: Scratch, Leer, Assurance, Dragon Rage, Dual Chop, Scary Face, Slash, False Swipe, Dragon Claw, Dragon Dance, Taunt, Dragon Pulse, Swords Dance, Guillotine, Outrage, Giga Impact

TYPE:
DRAGON

Fraxure clash in intense battles over territory. After a battle is over, they always remember to sharpen their tusks on smooth stones so they'll be ready for the next battle.

Axew → Fraxure → Haxorus

FROAKIE
Bubble Frog Pokémon

How to say it: FRO-kee

Height: 1' 00"   **Weight:** 15.4 lbs.

Possible Moves: Pound, Growl, Bubble, Quick Attack, Lick, Water Pulse, Smokescreen, Round, Fling, Smack Down, Substitute, Bounce, Double Team, Hydro Pump

The foamy bubbles that cover Froakie's body protect its sensitive skin from damage. It's always alert to any changes in its environment.

Froakie   Frogadier   Greninja

FROGADIER
Bubble Frog Pokémon

How to say it: FROG-uh-deer

Height: 2' 00"   **Weight:** 24.0 lbs.

Possible Moves: Pound, Growl, Bubble, Quick Attack, Lick, Water Pulse, Smokescreen, Round, Fling, Smack Down, Substitute, Bounce, Double Team, Hydro Pump

TYPE:
WATER

Swift and sure, Frogadier coats pebbles in a bubbly foam and then flings them with pinpoint accuracy. It has spectacular jumping and climbing skills.

Froakie   Frogadier   Greninja

FURFROU
Poodle Pokémon

How to say it: FUR-froo

Height: 3' 11"   **Weight:** 61.7 lbs.

Possible Moves: Tackle, Growl, Sand Attack, Baby-Doll Eyes, Headbutt, Tail Whip, Bite, Odor Sleuth, Retaliate, Take Down, Charm, Sucker Punch, Cotton Guard

An experienced groomer can trim Furfrou's fluffy coat into many different styles. Being groomed in this way makes the Pokémon both fancier and faster.

TYPE: NORMAL

Does not evolve

FURRET
Long Body Pokémon

TYPE:
NORMAL

How to say it: FUR-ret

Height: 5' 11"   **Weight:** 71.6 lbs.

Possible Moves: Scratch, Foresight, Defense Curl, Quick Attack, Fury Swipes, Helping Hand, Follow Me, Slam, Rest, Sucker Punch, Amnesia, Baton Pass, Me First, Hyper Voice

Because Furret are so long and thin, other Pokémon can't fit into their nests. In battle, they use their superior speed to outmaneuver opponents.

Sentret   Furret

GALLADE
Blade Pokémon

TYPE:
PSYCHIC-FIGHTING

How to say it: GAL-laid

Height: 5' 03"   **Weight:** 114.6 lbs.

Possible Moves: Stored Power, Close Combat, Leaf Blade, Night Slash, Leer, Confusion, Double Team, Teleport, Fury Cutter, Slash, Heal Pulse, Swords Dance, Psycho Cut, Helping Hand, Feint, False Swipe, Protect

A master of the blade, Gallade battles using the swordlike appendages that extend from its elbows.

Ralts   Kirlia   Gallade

GARDEVOIR

Embrace Pokémon

TYPE: PSYCHIC-FAIRY

How to say it: GAR-dee-VWAR

Height: 5' 03"   **Weight:** 106.7 lbs.

Possible Moves: Moonblast, Stored Power, Misty Terrain, Healing Wish, Growl, Confusion, Double Team, Teleport, Wish, Magical Leaf, Heal Pulse, Calm Mind, Psychic, Imprison, Future Sight, Captivate, Hypnosis, Dream Eater

Fiercely protective of its Trainer, Gardevoir wields its strongest psychic power if that Trainer is in danger. It can also see into the future.

MEGA GARDEVOIR

Embrace Pokémon

Height: 5' 03"
Weight: 106.7 lbs.

TYPE: PSYCHIC-FAIRY

Ralts   Kirlia   Gardevoir   Mega Gardevoir

GLOOM
Weed Pokémon

How to say it: GLOOM

Height: 2' 07"
Weight: 19.0 lbs.

Possible Moves: Absorb, Sweet Scent, Acid, Poison Powder, Stun Spore, Sleep Powder, Mega Drain, Lucky Chant, Natural Gift, Moonlight, Giga Drain, Petal Blizzard, Petal Dance, Grassy Terrain

Most people find the strong odor of Gloom's honey extremely unpleasant. But there's no accounting for taste—about one in a thousand will actually enjoy the way it smells.

TYPE:
GRASS-POISON

Oddish   Gloom   Vileplume

Bellossom

GOGOAT
Mount Pokémon

How to say it: GO-goat

Height: 5' 07"   **Weight:** 200.6 lbs.

Possible Moves: Aerial Ace, Tackle, Growth, Vine Whip, Tail Whip, Leech Seed, Razor Leaf, Worry Seed, Synthesis, Take Down, Bulldoze, Seed Bomb, Bulk Up, Double-Edge, Horn Leech, Leaf Blade, Milk Drink, Earthquake

This perceptive Pokémon can read its riders' feelings by paying attention to their grip on its horns. Gogoat also use their horns in battles for leadership.

TYPE:
GRASS

Skiddo   Gogoat

GOLBAT
Bat Pokémon

How to say it: GOL-bat

Height: 5' 03"
Weight: 121.3 lbs.

Possible Moves: Screech, Leech Life, Supersonic, Astonish, Bite, Wing Attack, Confuse Ray, Swift, Air Cutter, Acrobatics, Mean Look, Poison Fang, Haze, Air Slash

Golbat feeds on energy from living beings, biting with its huge mouth and sharp fangs. It won't stop until its victim is drained, even if it becomes so full that it can't fly.

TYPE:
POISON-FLYING

Zubat   Golbat   Crobat

GOLDEEN
Goldfish Pokémon

How to say it: GOL-deen

Height: 2' 00"
Weight: 33.1 lbs.

Possible Moves: Peck, Tail Whip, Water Sport, Supersonic, Horn Attack, Water Pulse, Flail, Aqua Ring, Fury Attack, Waterfall, Horn Drill, Agility, Soak, Megahorn

Because of the elegant waving of its graceful fins, Goldeen is known as the water dancer. It uses its horn for protection.

TYPE:
WATER

Goldeen   Seaking

GOLDUCK
Duck Pokémon

TYPE:
WATER

How to say it: GOL-duck

Height: 5' 07"   **Weight:** 168.9 lbs.

Possible Moves: Aqua Jet, Water Sport, Scratch, Tail Whip, Water Gun, Disable, Confusion, Water Pulse, Fury Swipes, Screech, Zen Headbutt, Aqua Tail, Soak, Psych Up, Amnesia, Hydro Pump, Wonder Room

Because of its webbed forelegs, Golduck is an excellent swimmer. When its forehead begins to glow, it can use its mystical powers.

Psyduck   Golduck

GRENINJA
Ninja Pokémon

How to say it: greh-NIN-jah

Height: 4' 11"
Weight: 88.2 lbs.

TYPE:
WATER-
DARK

Possible Moves: Night Slash, Role Play, Mat Block, Pound, Growl, Bubble, Quick Attack, Lick, Water Pulse, Smokescreen, Shadow Sneak, Spikes, Feint Attack, Water Shuriken, Substitute, Extrasensory, Double Team, Haze, Hydro Pump

Greninja can compress water into sharp-edged throwing stars. With the grace of a ninja, it slips in and out of sight to attack from the shadows.

Froakie   Frogadier   Greninja

How to say it: GULL-pin

Height: 1' 04"   **Weight:** 22.7 lbs.

Possible Moves: Pound, Yawn, Poison Gas, Sludge, Amnesia, Encore, Toxic, Acid Spray, Stockpile, Spit Up, Swallow, Belch, Sludge Bomb, Gastro Acid, Wring Out, Gunk Shot

Most of Gulpin's body is made up of its stomach, so its other organs are small. The powerful enzymes in its stomach can digest anything.

TYPE:
POISON

Gulpin   Swalot

GYARADOS

Atrocious Pokémon

How to say it: GARE-uh-dos

Height: 21' 04"   **Weight:** 518.1 lbs.

Possible Moves: Thrash, Bite, Dragon Rage, Leer, Twister, Ice Fang, Aqua Tail, Rain Dance, Hydro Pump, Dragon Dance, Hyper Beam

The enormous and violent Gyarados can destroy whole villages if it becomes enraged.

TYPE: WATER-FLYING

MEGA GYARADOS

Atrocious Pokémon

Height: 21' 04"
Weight: 672.4 lbs.

TYPE: WATER-DARK

Magikarp   Gyarados   Mega Gyarados

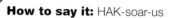

HAXORUS
Axe Jaw Pokémon

How to say it: HAK-soar-us

Height: 5' 11"   **Weight:** 232.6 lbs.

Possible Moves: Outrage, Scratch, Leer, Assurance, Dragon Rage, Dual Chop, Scary Face, Slash, False Swipe, Dragon Claw, Dragon Dance, Taunt, Dragon Pulse, Swords Dance, Guillotine, Giga Impact

Haxorus can cut through steel with its mighty tusks, which stay sharp no matter what. Its body is heavily armored.

TYPE:
DRAGON

Axew   Fraxure   Haxorus

HONEDGE
Sword Pokémon

How to say it: HONE-ej

Height: 2' 07"   **Weight:** 4.4 lbs.

Possible Moves: Tackle, Swords Dance, Fury Cutter, Metal Sound, Pursuit, Autotomize, Shadow Sneak, Aerial Ace, Retaliate, Slash, Iron Defense, Night Slash, Power Trick, Iron Head, Sacred Sword

Beware when approaching a Honedge! Those foolish enough to wield it like a sword will quickly find themselves wrapped in its blue cloth and drained of energy.

TYPE:
STEEL-
GHOST

Honedge   Doublade   Aegislash

HOPPIP
Cottonweed Pokémon

TYPE:
GRASS-
FLYING

How to say it: HOP-pip

Height: 1' 04"   **Weight:** 1.1 lbs.

Possible Moves: Splash, Synthesis, Tail Whip, Tackle, Fairy Wind, Poison Powder, Stun Spore, Sleep Powder, Bullet Seed, Leech Seed, Mega Drain, Acrobatics, Rage Powder, Cotton Spore, U-turn, Worry Seed, Giga Drain, Bounce, Memento

Hoppip's body is light enough to float on the wind. If it wants to stay on the ground, it has to hold on tightly with its feet. Large groups of Hoppip are said to be a sign of spring.

Hoppip   Skiploom   Jumpluff

ILLUMISE
Firefly Pokémon

TYPE:
BUG

How to say it: EE-loom-MEE-zay

Height: 2' 00"   **Weight:** 39.0 lbs.

Possible Moves: Tackle, Play Nice, Sweet Scent, Charm, Moonlight, Quick Attack, Wish, Encore, Flatter, Helping Hand, Zen Headbutt, Bug Buzz, Covet

Illumise gives off a sweet scent that attracts Volbeat by the dozen. It uses this scent to direct their light patterns.

Does not evolve

IVYSAUR
Seed Pokémon

How to say it: EYE-vee-sore

Height: 3' 03"   **Weight:** 28.7 lbs.

Possible Moves: Tackle, Growl, Leech Seed, Vine Whip, Poison Powder, Sleep Powder, Take Down, Razor Leaf, Sweet Scent, Growth, Double-Edge, Worry Seed, Synthesis, Solar Beam

When the flower bud on Ivysaur's back prepares to bloom, it swells and emits a sweet aroma.

Bulbasaur   Ivysaur   Venusaur    Mega Venusaur

TYPE:
GRASS-POISON

JUMPLUFF
Cottonweed Pokémon

How to say it: JUM-pluff

Height: 2' 07"   **Weight:** 6.6 lbs.

Possible Moves: Splash, Synthesis, Tail Whip, Tackle, Fairy Wind, Poison Powder, Stun Spore, Sleep Powder, Bullet Seed, Leech Seed, Mega Drain, Acrobatics, Rage Powder, Cotton Spore, U-turn, Worry Seed, Giga Drain, Bounce, Memento

While drifting on the breeze, Jumpluff can control its direction with its fluffy appendages. By doing this, it can travel anywhere the wind blows.

TYPE:
GRASS-
FLYING

Hoppip   Skiploom   Jumpluff

KADABRA
Psi Pokémon

TYPE:
POISON-
FLYING

How to say it: kuh-DAH-bra

Height: 4' 03"   **Weight:** 124.6 lbs.

Possible Moves: Teleport, Kinesis, Confusion, Disable, Miracle Eye, Ally Switch, Psybeam, Reflect, Telekinesis, Recover, Psycho Cut, Role Play, Psychic, Future Sight, Trick

The alpha waves Kadabra produces when it's using its powers can cause problems for nearby machinery.

Abra   Kadabra   Alakazam   Mega Alakazam

KAKUNA
Cocoon Pokémon

TYPE:
BUG-POISON

How to say it: kah-KOO-na

Height: 2' 00"   **Weight:** 22.0 lbs.

Possible Move: Harden

Inside its shell, Kakuna is almost immobile, so it hides in the trees. When in danger, it can make the shell harder to protect itself.

Weedle ➤ **Kakuna** ➤ **Beedrill**

KECLEON
Color Swap Pokémon

TYPE:
NORMAL

How to say it: KEH-clee-on

Height: 3' 03"   **Weight:** 48.5 lbs.

Possible Moves: Synchronoise, Ancient Power, Thief, Tail Whip, Astonish, Lick, Scratch, Bind, Feint Attack, Fury Swipes, Feint, Psybeam, Shadow Sneak, Slash, Screech, Substitute, Sucker Punch, Shadow Claw

A master of camouflage, Kecleon can alter its coloring to blend in with any surroundings. However, its zigzag pattern stays the same.

Does not evolve

KIRLIA
Emotion Pokémon

TYPE: PSYCHIC-FAIRY

How to say it: KERL-lee-ah

Height: 2' 07"
Weight: 44.5 lbs.

Possible Moves: Growl, Confusion, Double Team, Teleport, Lucky Chant, Magical Leaf, Heal Pulse, Calm Mind, Psychic, Imprison, Future Sight, Charm, Hypnosis, Dream Eater, Stored Power

Positive emotions send Kirlia into a joyful, spinning dance. It channels its Trainer's happiness into psychic power.

Ralts → Kirlia → Gardevoir → Mega Gardevoir

Gallade

LEDIAN
Five Star Pokémon

How to say it: LEH-dee-an

Height: 4' 07"   **Weight:** 78.5 lbs.

Possible Moves: Tackle, Supersonic, Comet Punch, Light Screen, Reflect, Safeguard, Mach Punch, Baton Pass, Silver Wind, Agility, Swift, Double-Edge, Bug Buzz

TYPE:
BUG-
FLYING

The pattern of Ledian's spots corresponds with the stars. As it flies through the night sky, it releases a powder that glows in the starlight.

Ledyba   Ledian

LEDYBA
Five Star Pokémon

TYPE:
BUG-
FLYING

How to say it: LEH-dee-bah

Height: 3' 03"   **Weight:** 23.8 lbs.

Possible Moves: Tackle, Supersonic, Comet Punch, Light Screen, Reflect, Safeguard, Mach Punch, Baton Pass, Silver Wind, Agility, Swift, Double-Edge, Bug Buzz

In cold weather, many Ledyba swarm to the same place, forming a big cluster to keep each other warm. These timid Pokémon also tend to stick together for protection.

Ledyba   Ledian

LINOONE
Rushing Pokémon

TYPE:
NORMAL

How to say it: line-NOON

Height: 1' 08"   **Weight:** 71.6 lbs.

Possible Moves: Play Rough, Rototiller, Switcheroo, Tackle, Growl, Tail Whip, Headbutt, Sand Attack, Odor Sleuth, Mud Sport, Fury Swipes, Covet, Bestow, Slash, Rest, Belly Drum, Fling

Although it can run faster than sixty miles an hour in a straight line, Linoone often has trouble navigating curves.

Zigzagoon ➡ Linoone

LITLEO
Lion Cub Pokémon

TYPE:
FIRE-
NORMAL

How to say it: LIT-lee-oh

Height: 2' 00"   **Weight:** 29.8 lbs.

Possible Moves: Tackle, Leer, Ember, Work Up, Headbutt, Noble Roar, Take Down, Fire Fang, Endeavor, Echoed Voice, Flamethrower, Crunch, Hyper Voice, Incinerate, Overheat

When Litleo is ready to get stronger, it leaves its pride to live alone. During a battle, its mane radiates intense heat.

Litleo ➡ Pyroar

TYPE: NORMAL

How to say it: LOUD-red

Height: 3' 03"   **Weight:** 89.3 lbs.

Possible Moves: Pound, Uproar, Astonish, Howl, Bite, Supersonic, Stomp, Screech, Roar, Synchronoise, Rest, Sleep Talk, Hyper Voice

A shout from a Loudred produces shock waves powerful enough to topple a big truck. When it starts stomping its feet, it's getting pumped up for battle.

Whismur → Loudred → Exploud

LUCARIO
Aura Pokémon

How to say it: loo-CAR-ee-oh

Height: 3' 11"
Weight: 119.0 lbs.

Possible Moves: Extreme Speed, Dragon Pulse, Close Combat, Aura Sphere, Foresight, Quick Attack, Detect, Metal Claw, Counter, Feint, Power-Up Punch, Swords Dance, Metal Sound, Bone Rush, Quick Guard, Me First, Calm Mind, Heal Pulse

Sensing the auras that all beings emanate allows Lucario to read minds and predict movements. Lucario is also very sensitive to others' emotions.

TYPE: FIGHTING-STEEL

MEGA LUCARIO
Aura Pokémon

Height: 4' 03"
Weight: 126.8 lbs.

TYPE: FIGHTING-STEEL

Riolu → Lucario → Mega Lucario

MAGIKARP

Fish Pokémon

How to say it: MADGE-eh-karp

Height: 2' 11"
Weight: 22.0 lbs.

Possible Moves: Splash, Tackle, Flail

Magikarp is widely regarded as the weakest Pokémon in the world. It lacks both speed and strength.

TYPE: WATER

Magikarp   Gyarados   Mega Gyarados

MARILL

Aqua Mouse Pokémon

How to say it: MARE-rull

Height: 1' 04"   **Weight:** 18.7 lbs.

TYPE: WATER-FAIRY

Possible Moves: Tackle, Water Gun, Tail Whip, Water Sport, Bubble, Defense Curl, Rollout, Bubble Beam, Helping Hand, Aqua Tail, Double-Edge, Aqua Ring, Rain Dance, Superpower, Hydro Pump, Play Rough

Marill's water-repelling fur keeps it dry even when it's playing in rivers and streams. Its buoyant tail lets it float with ease.

Azurill   Marill   Azumarill

MASQUERAIN

Eyeball Pokémon

TYPE:
BUG-
FLYING

How to say it: mas-ker-RAIN

Height: 2' 07"   **Weight:** 7.9 lbs.

Possible Moves: Quiver Dance, Bug Buzz, Whirlwind, Ominous Wind, Bubble, Quick Attack, Sweet Scent, Water Sport, Gust, Scary Face, Stun Spore, Silver Wind, Air Slash

The eye patterns on Masquerain's large antennae distract attackers. Its four wings let it fly in any direction, including sideways and backward, or hover in midair.

Surskit   Masquerain

MEDICHAM
Meditate Pokémon

TYPE:
FIGHTING-
PSYCHIC

How to say it: MED-uh-cham

Height: 4' 03"
Weight: 69.4 lbs.

Possible Moves: Zen Headbutt, Fire Punch, Thunder Punch, Ice Punch, Bide, Meditate, Confusion, Detect, Hidden Power, Mind Reader, Feint, Calm Mind, Force Palm, High Jump Kick, Psych Up, Acupressure, Power Trick, Reversal, Recover

Medicham can predict what its opponent will do next. It eludes the incoming attack with graceful movements, then strikes back.

MEGA MEDICHAM
Meditate Pokémon

Height: 4' 03"
Weight: 69.4 lbs.

TYPE:
FIGHTING-
PSYCHIC

Meditite   Medicham   Mega Medicham

MEDITITE

Meditate Pokémon

TYPE:
FIGHTING-
PSYCHIC

How to say it: MED-uh-tite

Height: 2' 00"   **Weight:** 24.7 lbs.

Possible Moves: Zen Headbutt, Fire Punch, Thunder Punch, Ice Punch, Bide, Meditate, Confusion, Detect, Hidden Power, Mind Reader, Feint, Calm Mind, Force Palm, High Jump Kick, Psych Up, Acupressure, Power Trick, Reversal, Recover

When Meditite levitates, it's using meditation to enhance its powers. Training in the mountains sharpens its focus.

Meditite   Medicham   Mega Medicham

MEOWSTIC
Constraint Pokémon

Male Form

Female Form

TYPE: PSYCHIC

How to say it: MYOW-stik

Height: 2' 00"   **Weight:** 18.7 lbs.

Possible Moves (male): Quick Guard, Mean Look, Helping Hand, Scratch, Leer, Covet, Confusion, Light Screen, Psybeam, Fake Out, Disarming Voice, Psyshock, Charm, Miracle Eye, Reflect, Psychic, Role Play, Imprison, Sucker Punch, Misty Terrain

Possible Moves (female): Stored Power, Me First, Magical Leaf, Scratch, Leer, Covet, Confusion, Light Screen, Psybeam, Fake Out, Disarming Voice, Psyshock, Charge Beam, Extrasensory, Psychic, Role Play, Signal Beam, Sucker Punch, Future Sight

When Meowstic unfolds its ears, the psychic blast created by the eyeball patterns inside can pulverize heavy machinery. It keeps its ears tightly folded unless it's in danger.

Espurr → Meowstic (Male Form)

Espurr → Meowstic (Female Form)

METAPOD
Cocoon Pokémon

TYPE:
BUG

How to say it: MET-uh-pod

Height: 2' 04"   **Weight:** 21.8 lbs.

Possible Move: Harden

While Metapod waits to evolve, its soft body is protected by a shell as hard as steel. The shell guards it from attacks and harsh conditions.

Caterpie   Metapod   Butterfree

MINUN
Cheering Pokémon

TYPE:
ELECTRIC

How to say it: MIE-nun

Height: 1' 04"   **Weight:** 9.3 lbs.

Possible Moves: Nasty Plot, Nuzzle, Entrainment, Play Nice, Growl, Thunder Wave, Quick Attack, Helping Hand, Spark, Encore, Charm, Copycat, Electro Ball, Swift, Fake Tears, Charge, Thunder, Baton Pass, Agility, Trump Card

Minun shoots out sparks to cheer on its friends. Being exposed to its electricity helps people relax and is good for their health.

Does not evolve

MOTHIM
Moth Pokémon

TYPE:
BUG-
FLYING

How to say it: MOTH-im

Height: 2' 11"
Weight: 51.4 lbs.

Possible Moves: Tackle, Protect, Bug Bite, Hidden Power, Confusion, Gust, Poison Powder, Psybeam, Camouflage, Silver Wind, Air Slash, Psychic, Bug Buzz, Quiver Dance

Mothim loves the taste of Combee's honey. Sometimes it will raid a hive at night to steal the sweet substance.

Burmy
(Male Form)   Mothim

MUNCHLAX
Big Eater Pokémon

TYPE:
NORMAL

How to say it: MUNCH-lax

Height: 2' 00"   **Weight:** 231.5 lbs.

Possible Moves: Last Resort, Snatch, Lick, Metronome, Odor Sleuth, Tackle, Defense Curl, Amnesia, Chip Away, Screech, Body Slam, Stockpile, Swallow, Rollout, Fling, Belly Drum, Natural Gift

Munchlax's long fur is a perfect place to hide snacks. With this permanent food stash, it never goes hungry.

Munchlax   Snorlax

NINCADA
Trainee Pokémon

How to say it: nin-KAH-da

Height: 1' 08"   **Weight:** 12.1 lbs.

Possible Moves: Scratch, Harden, Leech Life, Sand Attack, Fury Swipes, Mind Reader, False Swipe, Mud-Slap, Metal Claw, Dig

Nincada live underground, so their eyes aren't well developed. They use their antennae to sense their surroundings as they feed on tree roots.

TYPE:
BUG-
GROUND

Ninjask

Nincada

Shedinja

NINJASK
Ninja Pokémon

TYPE:
BUG-
FLYING

How to say it: NIN-jask

Height: 2' 07"   **Weight:** 26.5 lbs.

Possible Moves: Bug Bite, Scratch, Harden, Leech Life, Sand Attack, Fury Swipes, Mind Reader, Double Team, Fury Cutter, Screech, Swords Dance, Slash, Agility, Baton Pass, X-Scissor

At top speeds, Ninjask move so fast that they're hard to see. When they find a tree with delicious sap, they gather to feed.

Ninjask

Nincada

Shedinja

ODDISH
Weed Pokémon

TYPE: GRASS-POISON

How to say it: ODD-ish

Height: 1' 08"   **Weight:** 11.9 lbs.

Possible Moves: Absorb, Sweet Scent, Acid, Poison Powder, Stun Spore, Sleep Powder, Mega Drain, Lucky Chant, Natural Gift, Moonlight, Giga Drain, Petal Dance, Grassy Terrain

Oddish spends the day underground, out of the sun. After dark, it comes out to stretch its roots, go for a walk, and soak up the moonlight.

Vileplume

Oddish   Gloom

Bellossom

PANCHAM
Playful Pokémon

TYPE: FIGHTING

How to say it: PAN-chum

Height: 2' 00"   **Weight:** 17.6 lbs.

Possible Moves: Tackle, Leer, Arm Thrust, Work Up, Karate Chop, Comet Punch, Slash, Circle Throw, Vital Throw, Body Slam, Crunch, Entrainment, Parting Shot, Sky Uppercut

Pancham tries to be intimidating, but it's just too cute. When someone pats it on the head, it drops the tough-guy act and grins.

Pancham   Pangoro

PANGORO
Daunting Pokémon

TYPE:
FIGHTING-
DARK

How to say it: PAN-go-roh

Height: 6' 11"
Weight: 299.8 lbs.

Possible Moves: Entrainment, Hammer Arm, Tackle, Leer, Arm Thrust, Work Up, Karate Chop, Comet Punch, Slash, Circle Throw, Vital Throw, Body Slam, Crunch, Parting Shot, Sky Uppercut, Taunt, Low Sweep

The leafy sprig Pangoro holds in its mouth helps the Pokémon track its opponents' movements. Taking hits in battle doesn't seem to bother it at all.

Pancham ➡ Pangoro

PANPOUR
Spray Pokémon

TYPE:
WATER

How to say it: PAN-por

Height: 2' 00"
Weight: 29.8 lbs.

Possible Moves: Scratch, Play Nice, Leer, Lick, Water Gun, Fury Swipes, Water Sport, Bite, Scald, Taunt, Fling, Acrobatics, Brine, Recycle, Natural Gift, Crunch

Panpour's head tuft is full of nutrient-rich water. It uses its tail to water plants, which then grow big and healthy.

Panpour ➡ Simipour

PANSAGE

Grass Monkey Pokémon

TYPE:
GRASS

How to say it: PAN-sayj

Height: 2' 00"
Weight: 23.1 lbs.

Possible Moves: Scratch, Play Nice, Leer, Lick, Vine Whip, Fury Swipes, Leech Seed, Bite, Seed Bomb, Torment, Fling, Acrobatics, Grass Knot, Recycle, Natural Gift, Crunch

Chewing the leaf from Pansage's head is a known method of stress relief. It willingly shares its leaf—along with any berries it's collected—with those who need it.

Pansage Simisage

PANSEAR

High Temp Pokémon

How to say it: PAN-seer

Height: 2' 00"   **Weight:** 24.3 lbs

Possible Moves: Scratch, Play Nice, Leer, Lick, Incinerate, Fury Swipes, Yawn, Bite, Flame Burst, Amnesia, Fling, Acrobatics, Fire Blast, Recycle, Natural Gift, Crunch

Clever and helpful, Pansear prefers to cook its berries rather than eating them raw. Its natural habitat is volcanic caves, so it's no surprise that its fiery tuft burns at six hundred degrees Fahrenheit.

TYPE:
FIRE

Pansear Simisear

PICHU
Tiny Mouse Pokémon

How to say it: PEE-choo

Height: 1' 00"   **Weight:** 4.4 lbs.

Possible Moves: Thunder Shock, Charm, Tail Whip, Sweet Kiss, Thunder Wave, Nasty Plot

Pichu often play with one another by touching their tails together, creating a shower of electric sparks. They lack control over their own electricity and sometimes give off unexpected jolts.

TYPE:
ELECTRIC

Pichu   Pikachu   Raichu

PIDGEOT
Bird Pokémon

TYPE:
NORMAL-
FLYING

How to say it: PIDG-ee-ott

Height: 4' 11"   **Weight:** 87.1 lbs.

Possible Moves: Hurricane, Tackle, Sand Attack, Gust, Quick Attack, Whirlwind, Twister, Feather Dance, Agility, Wing Attack, Roost, Tailwind, Mirror Move, Air Slash

When in search of food, Pidgeot often swoop low over bodies of water, almost skimming the surface. They can fly faster than the speed of sound.

Pidgey   Pidgeotto   Pidgeot

PIDGEOTTO
Bird Pokémon

How to say it: PIDG-ee-OH-toe

Height: 3' 07"   **Weight:** 66.1 lbs

Possible Moves: Tackle, Sand Attack, Gust, Quick Attack, Whirlwind, Twister, Feather Dance, Agility, Wing Attack, Roost, Tailwind, Mirror Move, Air Slash, Hurricane

The territorial Pidgeotto goes after intruders with fierce blows of its beak. Its well-developed claws can hang on to an object over many miles of flight.

TYPE:
NORMAL-FLYING

Pidgey   Pidgeotto   Pidgeot

PIDGEY
Tiny Bird Pokémon

How to say it: PIDG-ee

Height: 1' 00"   **Weight:** 4.0 lbs.

Possible Moves: Tackle, Sand Attack, Gust, Quick Attack, Whirlwind, Twister, Feather Dance, Agility, Wing Attack, Roost, Tailwind, Mirror Move, Air Slash, Hurricane

Pidgey usually prefer not to fight unless they're disturbed. They stir up clouds of sand with their wings to make it harder for opponents to see them.

TYPE:
NORMAL-FLYING

Pidgey   Pidgeotto   Pidgeot

PIKACHU
Mouse Pokémon

TYPE:
ELECTRIC

How to say it: PEE-ka-choo

Height: 1' 04"
Weight: 13.2 lbs.

Possible Moves: Tail Whip, Thunder Shock, Growl, Play Nice, Quick Attack, Thunder Wave, Electro Ball, Double Team, Nuzzle, Slam, Thunderbolt, Feint, Agility, Discharge, Light Screen, Thunder

When threatened, Pikachu can deliver a powerful zap from the electric pouches on its cheeks. Its jagged tail sometimes attracts lightning during a storm.

Pichu   Pikachu   Raichu

PLUSLE
Cheering Pokémon

TYPE:
ELECTRIC

How to say it: PLUS-ull

Height: 1' 04"   **Weight:** 9.3 lbs.

Possible Moves: Nasty Plot, Nuzzle, Entrainment, Play Nice, Growl, Thunder Wave, Quick Attack, Helping Hand, Spark, Encore, Copycat, Electro Ball, Swift, Fake Tears, Charge, Thunder, Baton Pass, Agility, Last Resort

Plusle taps into telephone poles to drain their power. The pom-poms it waves when cheering for its friends are actually made of sparks.

Does not evolve

PSYDUCK
Duck Pokémon

TYPE:
WATER

How to say it: SY-duck

Height: 2' 07" **Weight:** 43.2 lbs.

Possible Moves: Water Sport, Scratch, Tail Whip, Water Gun, Disable, Confusion, Water Pulse, Fury Swipes, Screech, Zen Headbutt, Aqua Tail, Soak, Psych Up, Amnesia, Hydro Pump, Wonder Room

Psyduck is always suffering from a headache. The intensity of the headache amplifies its mystical powers.

Psyduck   Golduck

PYROAR
Royal Pokémon

How to say it: PIE-roar

Height: 4' 11" **Weight:** 179.7 lbs.

Possible Moves: Hyper Beam, Tackle, Leer, Ember, Work Up, Headbutt, Noble Roar, Take Down, Fire Fang, Endeavor, Echoed Voice, Flamethrower, Crunch, Hyper Voice, Incinerate, Overheat

Pyroar live together in prides, led by the male whose fiery mane is the biggest. The females of the pride guard the young.

Male Form

TYPE:
FIRE-
NORMAL

Female Form

Litleo   Pyroar

QUILLADIN
Spiny Armor Pokémon

How to say it: QUILL-uh-din

Height: 2' 04"   **Weight:** 63.9 lbs.

Possible Moves: Tackle, Growl, Vine Whip, Rollout, Bite, Leech Seed, Pin Missile, Needle Arm, Take Down, Seed Bomb, Mud Shot, Bulk Up, Body Slam, Pain Split, Wood Hammer

Quilladin often train for battle by charging forcefully into each other. Despite their spiky appearance, they have a gentle nature and don't like confrontation.

TYPE:
GRASS

Chespin   Quilladin   Chesnaught

RAICHU
Mouse Pokémon

TYPE:
ELECTRIC

How to say it: RYE-choo

Height: 2' 07"   **Weight:** 66.1 lbs.

Possible Moves: Thunder Shock, Tail Whip, Quick Attack, Thunderbolt

Raichu can take down much larger foes with high-voltage bursts of electricity. It gets twitchy and aggressive if its electricity is allowed to build up without release.

Pichu   Pikachu   Raichu

RALTS
Feeling Pokémon

TYPE:
PSYCHIC-FAIRY

How to say it: RALTS

Height: 1' 04"
Weight: 14.6 lbs.

Possible Moves: Growl, Confusion, Double Team, Teleport, Lucky Chant, Magical Leaf, Heal Pulse, Calm Mind, Psychic, Imprison, Future Sight, Charm, Hypnosis, Dream Eater, Stored Power

Ralts uses its pink horns to sense the emotions of those around it. Hostility sends it into hiding.

Ralts   Kirlia

Gardevoir   Mega Gardevoir

Gallade

RIOLU
Emanation Pokémon

TYPE:
FIGHTING

How to say it: ree-OH-loo

Height: 2' 04"
Weight: 44.5 lbs.

Possible Moves: Foresight, Quick Attack, Endure, Counter, Feint, Force Palm, Copycat, Screech, Reversal, Nasty Plot, Final Gambit

The aura surrounding Riolu's body indicates its emotional state. It alters the shape of this aura to communicate.

Riolu　　Lucario　　Mega Lucario

ROSELIA
Thorn Pokémon

How to say it: roh-ZEH-lee-uh

Height: 1' 00"　　**Weight:** 4.4 lbs.

Possible Moves: Absorb, Growth, Poison Sting, Stun Spore, Mega Drain, Leech Seed, Magical Leaf, Grass Whistle, Giga Drain, Toxic Spikes, Sweet Scent, Ingrain, Petal Dance, Toxic, Aromatherapy, Synthesis, Petal Blizzard

When a Roselia blooms in an unusual color, it's a sign that it's been drinking from a mineral-rich spring. Its hands secrete two different kinds of poison.

TYPE:
GRASS-
POISON

Budew　　Roselia　　Roserade

ROSERADE
Bouquet Pokémon

TYPE:
GRASS-
POISON

How to say it: ROSE-raid

Height: 2' 11"   **Weight:** 32.0 lbs.

Possible Moves: Venom Drench, Grassy Terrain, Weather Ball, Poison Sting, Mega Drain, Magical Leaf, Sweet Scent

With its beautiful blooms, enticing aroma, and graceful movements, Roserade is quite enchanting—but watch out! Its arms conceal thorny whips, and the thorns carry poison.

Budew   Roselia   Roserade

SCATTERBUG
Scatterdust Pokémon

How to say it: SCAT-ter-BUG

Height: 1' 00"   **Weight:** 5.5 lbs.

Possible Moves: Tackle, String Shot, Stun Spore, Bug Bite

When threatened, Scatterbug protects itself with a cloud of black powder that can paralyze its attacker. This powder also serves as protection from the elements.

TYPE:
BUG

Scatterbug   Spewpa   Vivillon

SCOLIPEDE

Megapede Pokémon

TYPE:
BUG-
POISON

How to say it: SKOH-lih-peed

Height: 8' 02"   **Weight:** 442.0 lbs.

Possible Moves: Megahorn, Defense Curl, Rollout, Poison Sting, Screech, Pursuit, Protect, Poison Tail, Bug Bite, Venoshock, Baton Pass, Agility, Steamroller, Toxic, Venom Drench, Rock Climb, Double-Edge

The claws near Scolipede's head can be used to grab, immobilize, and poison its opponent. Scolipede Moves quickly when chasing down enemies.

Venipede   Whirlipede   Scolipede

SCRAFTY

Hoodlum Pokémon

TYPE:
DARK-
FIGHTING

How to say it: SKRAF-tee

Height: 3' 07"   **Weight:** 66.1 lbs.

Possible Moves: Leer, Low Kick, Sand Attack, Feint Attack, Headbutt, Swagger, Brick Break, Payback, Chip Away, High Jump Kick, Scary Face, Crunch, Facade, Rock Climb, Focus Punch, Head Smash

A group of Scrafty is led by the one with the biggest crest. Their powerful kicks can shatter concrete.

Scraggy   Scrafty

SCRAGGY
Shedding Pokémon

How to say it: SKRAG-ee

Height: 2' 00"　**Weight:** 26.0 lbs.

Possible Moves: Leer, Low Kick, Sand Attack, Feint Attack, Headbutt, Swagger, Brick Break, Payback, Chip Away, High Jump Kick, Scary Face, Crunch, Facade, Rock Climb, Focus Punch, Head Smash

Scraggy can pull its loose, rubbery skin up around its neck to protect itself from attacks. With its tough skull, it delivers headbutts without warning.

TYPE:
DARK-FIGHTING

Scraggy　Scrafty

SEAKING
Goldfish Pokémon

TYPE:
WATER

How to say it: SEE-king

Height: 4' 03"　**Weight:** 86.0 lbs.

Possible Moves: Megahorn, Poison Jab, Peck, Tail Whip, Water Sport, Supersonic, Horn Attack, Water Pulse, Flail, Aqua Ring, Fury Attack, Waterfall, Horn Drill, Agility, Soak

Using its powerful horn, Seaking can carve out holes in river rocks to make a nest. It swims upstream during the autumn.

Goldeen　Seaking

SENTRET
Scout Pokémon

TYPE:
NORMAL

How to say it: SEN-tret

Height: 2' 07"
Weight: 13.2 lbs.

Possible Moves: Scratch, Foresight, Defense Curl, Quick Attack, Fury Swipes, Helping Hand, Follow Me, Slam, Rest, Sucker Punch, Amnesia, Baton Pass, Me First, Hyper Voice

Sentret keep a careful eye on their surroundings, often standing up high on their tails so they can see farther. They also use their tails to drum on the ground as a warning.

Sentret   Furret

SHARPEDO
Brutal Pokémon

TYPE:
WATER-
DARK

How to say it: shar-PEE-do

Height: 5' 11"   **Weight:** 195.8 lbs.

Possible Moves: Night Slash, Feint, Leer, Bite, Rage, Focus Energy, Scary Face, Ice Fang, Screech, Swagger, Assurance, Crunch, Slash, Aqua Jet, Taunt, Agility, Skull Bash

Sharpedo can pierce thick sheet metal with its teeth. Its streamlined body can cut through the water at seventy-five miles per hour.

Carvanha   Sharpedo

SHEDINJA
Shed Pokémon

TYPE:
BUG-GHOST

How to say it: sheh-DIN-ja

Height: 2' 07"   **Weight:** 2.6 lbs.

Possible Moves: Scratch, Harden, Leech Life, Sand Attack, Fury Swipes, Mind Reader, Spite, Confuse Ray, Shadow Sneak, Grudge, Phantom Force, Heal Block, Shadow Ball

Some believe that looking into the crack on Shedinja's back puts your spirit in danger. Under certain circumstances, it appears alongside Ninjask when Nincada evolves.

Ninjask

Nincada

Shedinja

SIMIPOUR
Geyser Pokémon

How to say it: SIH-mee-por

Height: 3' 03"
Weight: 63.9 lbs.

Possible Moves: Leer, Lick, Fury Swipes, Scald

Simipour can shoot water out of its tail with such force that it can punch right through a concrete wall. When its stores run low, it dips its tail into clean water to suck up a refill.

TYPE:
WATER

Panpour   Simipour

SIMISAGE
Thorn Monkey Pokémon

TYPE:
GRASS

How to say it: SIH-mee-sayj

Height: 3' 07"
Weight: 67.2 lbs.

Possible Moves: Leer, Lick, Fury Swipes, Seed Bomb

Simisage's tail is covered in thorns, and it uses the tail like a whip to lash out at opponents. It always seems to be in a bad mood.

Pansage   Simisage

SIMISEAR
Ember Pokémon

How to say it: SIH-mee-seer

Height: 3' 03"
Weight: 61.7 lbs.

Possible Moves: Leer, Lick, Fury Swipes, Flame Burst

Simisear's head and tail give off embers in the heat of battle . . . or any time it's excited. It has quite a sweet tooth.

TYPE:
FIRE

Pansear   Simisear

SKIDDO
Mount Pokémon

TYPE:
GRASS

How to say it: skid-OO

Height: 2' 11"　**Weight:** 68.3 lbs.

Possible Moves: Tackle, Growth, Vine Whip, Tail Whip, Leech Seed, Razor Leaf, Worry Seed, Synthesis, Take Down, Bulldoze, Seed Bomb, Bulk Up, Double-Edge, Horn Leech, Leaf Blade, Milk Drink

Calm and gentle, Skiddo have been living side by side with people for many generations. They can create energy via photosynthesis.

Skiddo　　Gogoat

SKIPLOOM
Cottonweed Pokémon

How to say it: SKIP-loom

Height: 2' 00"　**Weight:** 2.2 lbs.

TYPE:
GRASS-
FLYING

Possible Moves: Splash, Synthesis, Tail Whip, Tackle, Fairy Wind, Poison Powder, Stun Spore, Sleep Powder, Bullet Seed, Leech Seed, Mega Drain, Acrobatics, Rage Powder, Cotton Spore, U-turn, Worry Seed, Giga Drain, Bounce, Memento

Skiploom opens its petals wide to soak up the sun. The blossom on its head responds to temperature, closing up when it's cold.

Hoppip　　Skiploom　　Jumpluff

SKITTY
Kitten Pokémon

TYPE:
NORMAL

How to say it: SKIT-tee

Height: 2' 00"
Weight: 24.3 lbs.

Possible Moves: Fake Out, Growl, Tail Whip, Tackle, Foresight, Attract, Sing, Double Slap, Copycat, Assist, Charm, Feint Attack, Wake-Up Slap, Covet, Heal Bell, Double-Edge, Captivate, Play Rough

Anything that moves draws Skitty's attention and starts a playful game of chase. It often chases its own tail in a dizzying circle.

Skitty   →   Delcatty

SLURPUFF
Meringue Pokémon

TYPE:
FAIRY

How to say it: SLUR-puff

Height: 2' 07" **Weight:** 11.0 lbs.

Possible Moves: Sweet Scent, Tackle, Fairy Wind, Play Nice, Fake Tears, Round, Cotton Spore, Endeavor, Aromatherapy, Draining Kiss, Energy Ball, Cotton Guard, Wish, Play Rough, Light Screen, Safeguard

Pastry chefs love having a Slurpuff in the kitchen. With its incredibly sensitive nose, it can tell exactly when a dessert is baked to perfection.

Swirlix   →   Slurpuff

SMEARGLE
Painter Pokémon

How to say it: SMEAR-gull

Height: 3' 11"   **Weight:** 127.9 lbs.

Possible Moves: Sketch

Smeargle use their tails like paintbrushes to draw thousands of different territorial markings. The footprints on their backs were left there by fellow Smeargle.

TYPE:
NORMAL

Does not evolve

SNORLAX
Sleeping Pokémon

TYPE:
NORMAL

How to say it: SNOR-lacks

Height: 6' 11"   **Weight:** 1,014.1 lbs.

Possible Moves: Tackle, Defense Curl, Amnesia, Lick, Chip Away, Yawn, Body Slam, Rest, Snore, Sleep Talk, Rollout, Block, Belly Drum, Crunch, Heavy Slam, Giga Impact

Snorlax spends most of its time eating and sleeping. Its impressive powers of digestion are unfazed by mold or rot on the food it eats.

Munchlax   Snorlax

SPEWPA
Scatterdust Pokémon

How to say it: SPEW-puh

Height: 1' 00"   **Weight:** 18.5 lbs.

Possible Moves: Harden, Protect

Like Scatterbug, Spewpa releases a protective cloud of powder when attacked. It can also bristle up its thick fur in an attempt to scare off any aggressors.

TYPE:
BUG

Scatterbug   Spewpa   Vivillon

SPRITZEE
Perfume Pokémon

TYPE:
FAIRY

How to say it: SPRIT-zee

Height: 0' 08"   **Weight:** 1.1 lbs.

Possible Moves: Sweet Scent, Fairy Wind, Sweet Kiss, Odor Sleuth, Echoed Voice, Calm Mind, Draining Kiss, Aromatherapy, Attract, Moonblast, Charm, Flail, Misty Terrain, Skill Swap, Psychic, Disarming Voice

Long ago, this Pokémon was popular among the nobility for its lovely scent. Instead of spraying perfume, ladies would keep a Spritzee close at hand.

Spritzee   Aromatisse

SQUIRTLE
Tiny Turtle Pokémon

How to say it: SKWIR-tul

Height: 1' 08"   **Weight:** 19.8 lbs.

Possible Moves: Tackle, Tail Whip, Water Gun, Withdraw, Bubble, Bite, Rapid Spin, Protect, Water Pulse, Aqua Tail, Skull Bash, Iron Defense, Rain Dance, Hydro Pump

Squirtle hides in its shell for protection, but it can still fight back. Whenever it sees an opening, it strikes at its foe with spouts of water.

Squirtle   Wartortle   Blastoise   Mega Blastoise

TYPE:
WATER

SURSKIT
Pond Skater Pokémon

How to say it: SUR-skit

Height: 1' 08"   **Weight:** 3.7 lbs.

Possible Moves: Bubble, Quick Attack, Sweet Scent, Water Sport, Bubble Beam, Agility, Mist, Haze, Baton Pass, Sticky Web

When Surskit move across the surface of the water, they look like they're on skates. Sometimes they can be seen skating on puddles after a rainstorm.

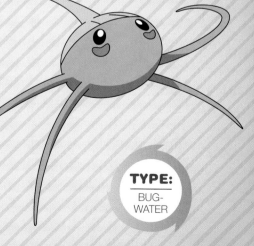

Surskit   Masquerain

TYPE:
BUG-
WATER

SWALOT

Poison Bag Pokémon

TYPE: POISON

How to say it: SWAH-lot

Height: 5' 07"   **Weight:** 176.4 lbs.

Possible Moves: Gunk Shot, Wring Out, Pound, Yawn, Poison Gas, Sludge, Amnesia, Encore, Body Slam, Toxic, Acid Spray, Stockpile, Spit Up, Swallow, Belch, Sludge Bomb, Gastro Acid

Swalot's mouth can open wide enough to swallow its food whole. When under attack, it sweats heavily, covering its opponent in the poisonous fluid.

Gulpin ➜ Swalot

SWANNA

White Bird Pokémon

TYPE: WATER-FLYING

How to say it: SWAH-nuh

Height: 4' 03"   **Weight:** 53.4 lbs.

Possible Moves: Water Gun, Water Sport, Defog, Wing Attack, Water Pulse, Aerial Ace, Bubble Beam, Feather Dance, Aqua Ring, Air Slash, Roost, Rain Dance, Tailwind, Brave Bird, Hurricane

In the evening, a flock of Swanna performs an elegant dance around its leader. Their exceptional stamina and wing strength allow them to fly thousands of miles at a time.

Ducklett ➜ Swanna

SWIRLIX
Cotton Candy Pokémon

TYPE: FAIRY

How to say it: SWUR-licks

Height: 1' 04"   **Weight:** 7.7 lbs.

Possible Moves: Sweet Scent, Tackle, Fairy Wind, Play Nice, Fake Tears, Round, Cotton Spore, Endeavor, Aromatherapy, Draining Kiss, Energy Ball, Cotton Guard, Wish, Play Rough, Light Screen, Safeguard

Swirlix loves to snack on sweets. Its sugary eating habits have made its white fur sweet and sticky, just like cotton candy.

Swirlix   Slurpuff

TALONFLAME
Scorching Pokémon

How to say it: TAL-un-flame

Height: 3' 11"   **Weight:** 54.0 lbs.

Possible Moves: Brave Bird, Flare Blitz, Tackle, Growl, Quick Attack, Peck, Agility, Flail, Ember, Roost, Razor Wind, Natural Gift, Flame Charge, Acrobatics, Me First, Tailwind, Steel Wing

Talonflame can swoop at incredible speeds when attacking. During intense battles, its wings give off showers of embers as it flies.

TYPE: FIRE-FLYING

Fletchling Fletchinder Talonflame

TOXICROAK

Toxic Mouth Pokémon

TYPE:
POISON-
FIGHTING

How to say it: TOX-uh-croak

Height: 4' 03"   **Weight:** 97.9 lbs.

Possible Moves: Astonish, Mud-Slap, Poison Sting, Taunt, Pursuit, Feint Attack, Revenge, Swagger, Mud Bomb, Sucker Punch, Venoshock, Nasty Plot, Poison Jab, Sludge Bomb, Belch, Flatter

Toxicroak's dangerous poison is stored in its throat sac and delivered through the claws on its knuckles.

Croagunk   Toxicroak

VENIPEDE

Centipede Pokémon

How to say it: VEHN-ih-peed

Height: 1' 04"   **Weight:** 11.7 lbs.

Possible Moves: Defense Curl, Rollout, Poison Sting, Screech, Pursuit, Protect, Poison Tail, Bug Bite, Venoshock, Agility, Steamroller, Toxic, Rock Climb, Double-Edge

Venipede uses the feelers at both ends of its body to explore its surroundings. It's extremely aggressive, and its bite is poisonous.

TYPE:
BUG-
POISON

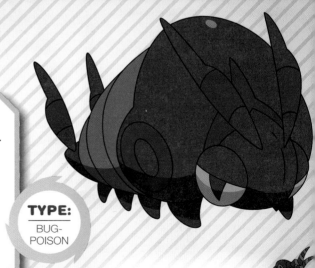

Venipede   Whirlipede   Scolipede

VENUSAUR
Seed Pokémon

How to say it: VEE-nuh-sore

Height: 6' 07"
Weight: 220.5 lbs.

Possible Moves: Tackle, Growl, Vine Whip, Leech Seed, Poison Powder, Sleep Powder, Take Down, Razor Leaf, Sweet Scent, Growth, Double-Edge, Petal Dance, Worry Seed, Synthesis, Petal Blizzard, Solar Beam

The scent of the flower on Venusaur's back intensifies after a rainy day. Other Pokémon are drawn to this fragrance.

TYPE:
GRASS-POISON

MEGA VENUSAUR
Seed Pokémon

Height: 7' 10"
Weight: 342.8 lbs.

TYPE:
GRASS-POISON

Bulbasaur → **Ivysaur** → **Venusaur** → **Mega Venusaur**

VESPIQUEN
Beehive Pokémon

TYPE:
BUG-
FLYING

How to say it: VES-pih-kwen

Height: 3' 11"   **Weight:** 84.9 lbs.

Possible Moves: Fell Stinger, Destiny Bond, Sweet Scent, Gust, Poison Sting, Confuse Ray, Fury Cutter, Pursuit, Fury Swipes, Defend Order, Slash, Power Gem, Heal Order, Toxic, Air Slash, Captivate, Attack Order, Swagger

Vespiquen controls the colony that lives in its honeycomb body by releasing pheromones. It feeds the colony with honey provided by Combee.

Combee ➡ Vespiquen

VILEPLUME
Flower Pokémon

How to say it: VILE-ploom

Height: 3' 11"   **Weight:** 41.0 lbs.

Possible Moves: Mega Drain, Aromatherapy, Stun Spore, Poison Powder, Petal Blizzard, Petal Dance, Solar Beam

Vileplume's enormous petals release clouds of poisonous pollen as it walks. Bigger petals hold larger stores of this toxic pollen.

TYPE:
GRASS-
POISON

Oddish ➡ Gloom ➡ Vileplume

Bellossom

TYPE:
BUG-
FLYING

How to say it: VIH-vee-yon

Height: 3' 11"   **Weight:** 37.5 lbs.

Possible Moves: Powder, Sleep Powder, Poison Powder, Stun Spore, Gust, Light Screen, Struggle Bug, Psybeam, Supersonic, Draining Kiss, Aromatherapy, Bug Buzz, Safeguard, Quiver Dance, Hurricane

The colorful patterns on Vivillon's wings are determined by the Pokémon's habitat. Vivillon from different parts of the world have different wing patterns.

Scatterbug ➡ Spewpa ➡ Vivillon

VOLBEAT
Firefly Pokémon

How to say it: VOLL-beat

Height: 2' 04"
Weight: 39.0 lbs.

Possible Moves: Flash, Tackle, Double Team, Confuse Ray, Moonlight, Quick Attack, Tail Glow, Signal Beam, Protect, Helping Hand, Zen Headbutt, Bug Buzz, Double-Edge

Volbeat flashes the light on its tail to send messages to others at night. The scent of Illumise makes it very happy.

TYPE:
BUG

Does not evolve

WARTORTLE
Turtle Pokémon

TYPE:
WATER

How to say it: WOR-TORE-tul

Height: 3' 03"   **Weight:** 49.6 lbs.

Possible Moves: Tackle, Tail Whip, Water Gun, Withdraw, Bubble, Bite, Rapid Spin, Protect, Water Pulse, Aqua Tail, Skull Bash, Iron Defense, Rain Dance, Hydro Pump

Wartortle's furry tail is a popular longevity symbol—this Pokémon is said to live as long as ten thousand years.

Squirtle   Wartortle   Blastoise   Mega Blastois

WEEDLE
Hairy Bug Pokémon

How to say it: WEE-dull

Height: 1' 00"   **Weight:** 7.1 lbs.

Possible Moves: Poison Sting, String Shot, Bug Bite

The two-inch barb on top of Weedle's head is a powerful poisonous stinger. Weedle lives in wooded areas or open fields.

TYPE:
BUG-
POISON

Weedle   Kakuna   Beedrill

WHIRLIPEDE
Curlipede Pokémon

How to say it: WHIR-lih-peed

Height: 3' 11"   **Weight:** 129.0 lbs.

Possible Moves: Defense Curl, Rollout, Poison Sting, Screech, Pursuit, Protect, Poison Tail, Iron Defense, Bug Bite, Venoshock, Agility, Steamroller, Toxic, Venom Drench, Rock Climb, Double-Edge

Covered in a sturdy shell, Whirlipede doesn't move much unless it's attacked. Then it leaps into action, spinning at high velocity and smashing into the attacker.

TYPE:
BUG-
POISON

Venipede   Whirlipede   Scolipede

WHISMUR
Whisper Pokémon

TYPE:
NORMAL

How to say it: WHIS-mur

Height: 2' 00"   **Weight:** 35.9 lbs.

Possible Moves: Pound, Uproar, Astonish, Howl, Supersonic, Stomp, Screech, Roar, Synchronoise, Rest, Sleep Talk, Hyper Voice

When threatened, Whismur drives the attacker away with a cry as loud as a jet engine. It becomes quiet when the covers on its ears are closed.

Whismur → Loudred → Exploud

WORMADAM (PLANT CLOAK)
Bagworm Pokémon

TYPE:
BUG-GRASS

How to say it: WUR-muh-dam

Height: 1' 08"   **Weight:** 14.3 lbs.

Possible Moves: Tackle, Protect, Bug Bite, Hidden Power, Confusion, Razor Leaf, Growth, Psybeam, Captivate, Flail, Attract, Psychic, Leaf Storm

The cloak it wore as Burmy becomes a permanent part of Wormadam's body. Its appearance is determined by its surroundings at the time of Evolution.

Burmy (Female Form) → Wormadam

WORMADAM (SANDY CLOAK)

Bagworm Pokémon

How to say it: WUR-muh-dam

Height: 1' 08"   **Weight:** 14.3 lbs.

Possible Moves: Tackle, Protect, Bug Bite, Hidden Power, Confusion, Rock Blast, Harden, Psybeam, Captivate, Flail, Attract, Psychic, Fissure

If you want a Bug- and Ground-type Wormadam, make sure your Burmy has a Sandy Cloak! Once Burmy evolves, there's no going back.

TYPE:
BUG-GROUND

Burmy
(male Form)   **Wormadam**

WORMADAM (TRASH CLOAK)

Bagworm Pokémon

How to say it: WUR-muh-dam

Height: 1' 08"   **Weight:** 14.3 lbs.

Possible Moves: Tackle, Protect, Bug Bite, Hidden Power, Confusion, Mirror Shot, Metal Sound, Psybeam, Captivate, Flail, Attract, Psychic, Iron Head

Looking for a Wormadam with awesome Steel-type Moves? You'll need to evolve a Burmy with a Trash Cloak.

Burmy
(Female Form)   **Wormadam**

ZIGZAGOON

TinyRaccoon Pokémon

TYPE:
NORMAL

How to say it: ZIG-zag-GOON

Height: 1' 04"
Weight: 38.6 lbs.

Possible Moves: Growl, Tackle, Tail Whip, Headbutt, Baby-Doll Eyes, Sand Attack, Odor Sleuth, Mud Sport, Pin Missile, Covet, Bestow, Flail, Rest, Belly Drum, Fling

The curious and easily distracted Zigzagoon walks in a distinctive zigzag pattern because it's always dashing off to check out any item it spots in the grass.

Zigzagoon   Linoone

ZUBAT

Bat Pokémon

TYPE:
POISON-
FLYING

How to say it: ZOO-bat

Height: 2' 07" **Weight:** 16.5 lbs.

Possible Moves: Leech Life, Supersonic, Astonish, Bite, Wing Attack, Confuse Ray, Swift, Air Cutter, Acrobatics, Mean Look, Poison Fang, Haze, Air Slash

Zubat live in dark caves, where they find their way with echolocation, bouncing their ultrasonic cries off nearby objects to sense their surroundings. They have no eyes.

Zubat   Golbat   Crobat

Welcome to the Kalos Coastal Subregion!

Whether you prefer the shore or the sea, you're sure to find interesting Pokémon in the Coastal Kalos subregion. You'll find lots of Water-type Pokémon here—and sandy Ground-type and Rock-type Pokémon, too! Wingull, Tentacool, and Staryu are plentiful here, as are Onix, Tyrunt, Rhydon, and Krookodile.

ABSOL
Disaster Pokémon

TYPE:
DARK

How to say it: AB-sol

Height: 3' 11"
Weight: 103.6 lbs.

Possible Moves: Perish Song, Me First, Razor Wind, Detect, Taunt, Scratch, Feint, Leer, Quick Attack, Pursuit, Bite, Double Team, Slash, Swords Dance, Future Sight, Night Slash, Detect, Psycho Cut, Sucker Punch

Where Absol appears, disaster often follows. Rather than heed its warning, people sometimes blame it for whatever happens next.

MEGA ABSOL
Disaster Pokémon

Height: 3' 11"
Weight: 108.0 lbs.

TYPE:
DARK

Absol   Mega Absol

AERODACTYL

Fossil Pokémon

How to say it: AIR-row-DACK-tull

Height: 5' 11"
Weight: 130.1 lbs.

Possible Moves: Iron Head, Ice Fang, Fire Fang, Thunder Fang, Wing Attack, Supersonic, Bite, Scary Face, Roar, Agility, Ancient Power, Crunch, Take Down, Sky Drop, Hyper Beam, Rock Slide, Giga Impact

This Pokémon was restored from an ancient piece of amber. As Aerodactyl flies, it screeches in a high-pitched voice.

TYPE:
ROCK-
FLYING

MEGA AERODACTYL

Fossil Pokémon

Height: 6' 11"
Weight: 174.2 lbs.

TYPE:
ROCK-
FLYING

Aerodactyl   **Mega Aerodactyl**

ALOMOMOLA
Caring Pokémon

How to say it: uh-LOH-muh-MOH-luh

Height: 3' 11"   **Weight:** 69.7 lbs.

Possible Moves: Hydro Pump, Wide Guard, Healing Wish, Pound, Water Sport, Aqua Ring, Aqua Jet, Double Slap, Heal Pulse, Protect, Water Pulse, Wake-Up Slap, Soak, Wish, Brine, Safeguard, Helping Hand

When Alomomola finds injured Pokémon in the open sea where it lives, it gently wraps its healing fins around them and guides them to shore.

TYPE:
WATER

Does not evolve

AMAURA
Tundra Pokémon

TYPE:
ROCK-
ICE

How to say it: ah-MORE-uh

Height: 4' 03"
Weight: 55.6 lbs.

Possible Moves: Growl, Powder Snow, Thunder Wave, Rock Throw, Icy Wind, Take Down, Mist, Aurora Beam, Ancient Power, Round, Avalanche, Hail, Nature Power, Encore, Light Screen, Ice Beam, Hyper Beam, Blizzard

In the ancient world, Amaura's cold habitat kept predators at bay. It was restored from a frozen fragment.

Amaura   Aurorus

AMPHAROS

Light Pokémon

How to say it: AMF-fah-rahs

Height: 4' 07"   **Weight:** 135.6 lbs.

Possible Moves: Zap Cannon, Magnetic Flux, Ion Deluge, Dragon Pulse, Fire Punch, Tackle, Growl, Thunder Wave, Thunder Shock, Cotton Spore, Charge, Take Down, Electro Ball, Confuse Ray, Thunder Punch, Power Gem, Discharge, Cotton Guard, Signal Beam, Light Screen, Thunder

Ampharos shines a bright light from the tip of its tail. Wandering travelers can see the light from far away and follow it to safety.

MEGA AMPHAROS

Light Pokémon

Height: 4' 07"
Weight: 135.6 lbs.

TYPE:
ELECTRIC-
DRAGON

Mareep   Flaaffy   Ampharos   Mega Ampharos

ARTICUNO
Freeze Pokémon

LEGENDARY POKÉMON

TYPE:
ICE-
FLYING

How to say it: ART-tick-COO-no

Height: 5' 07"   **Weight:** 122.1 lbs.

Possible Moves: Roost, Hurricane, Freeze-Dry, Tailwind, Sheer Cold, Gust, Powder Snow, Mist, Ice Shard, Mind Reader, Ancient Power, Agility, Ice Beam, Reflect, Hail, Blizzard

It is said that doomed travelers sometimes see Articuno in the mountains. This Legendary Pokémon can freeze water vapor in the air.

Does not evolve

AURORUS
Tundra Pokémon

TYPE:
ROCK-
ICE

How to say it: ah-ROAR-us

Height: 8' 10"
Weight: 496.0 lbs.

Possible Moves: Freeze-Dry, Growl, Powder Snow, Thunder Wave, Rock Throw, Icy Wind, Take Down, Mist, Aurora Beam, Ancient Power, Round, Avalanche, Hail, Nature Power, Encore, Light Screen, Ice Beam, Hyper Beam, Blizzard

With the icy crystals that line its sides, Aurorus can freeze the surrounding air and trap its foes in ice.

Amaura   Aurorus

BAGON
Rock Head Pokémon

How to say it: BAY-gon

Height: 2' 00"
Weight: 92.8 lbs.

Possible Moves: Rage, Bite, Leer, Headbutt, Focus Energy, Ember, Dragon Breath, Zen Headbutt, Scary Face, Crunch, Dragon Claw, Double-Edge

Looking forward to the day it will be able to fly, Bagon practices by jumping from high places.

TYPE: DRAGON

Bagon   Shelgon   Salamence

BARBARACLE
Collective Pokémon

How to say it: bar-BARE-uh-kull

Height: 4' 03"
Weight: 211.6 lbs.

Possible Moves: Stone Edge, Skull Bash, Shell Smash, Scratch, Sand Attack, Water Gun, Withdraw, Fury Swipes, Slash, Mud-Slap, Clamp, Rock Polish, Ancient Power, Hone Claws, Fury Cutter, Night Slash, Razor Shell, Cross Chop

When seven Binacle come together to fight as one, a Barbaracle is formed. The head gives the orders, but the limbs don't always listen.

TYPE: ROCK-WATER

Binacle   Barbaracle

BINACLE
Two-Handed Pokémon

TYPE:
ROCK-WATER

How to say it: BY-nuh-kull

Height: 1' 08"   **Weight:** 68.3 lbs.

Possible Moves: Shell Smash, Scratch, Sand Attack, Water Gun, Withdraw, Fury Swipes, Slash, Mud-Slap, Clamp, Rock Polish, Ancient Power, Hone Claws, Fury Cutter, Night Slash, Razor Shell, Cross Chop

Binacle live in pairs, two on the same rock. They comb the beach for seaweed to eat.

Binacle   Barbaracle

BOLDORE
Ore Pokémon

TYPE:
ROCK

How to say it: BOHL-dohr

Height: 2' 11"   **Weight:** 224.9 lbs.

Possible Moves: Tackle, Harden, Sand Attack, Headbutt, Rock Blast, Mud-Slap, Iron Defense, Smack Down, Power Gem, Rock Slide, Stealth Rock, Sandstorm, Stone Edge, Explosion

The energy within Boldore's body overflows, leaks out, and forms into orange crystals. Though its head always points in the same direction, it can quickly move sideways and backward.

Roggenrola   Boldore   Gigalith

CARBINK
Jewel Pokémon

How to say it: CAR-bink

Height: 1' 0"
Weight: 12.6 lbs.

Possible Moves: Tackle, Harden, Rock Throw, Sharpen, Smack Down, Reflect, Stealth Rock, Guard Split, Ancient Power, Flail, Skill Swap, Power Gem, Stone Edge, Moonblast, Light Screen, Safeguard

While excavating caves, miners and archeologists sometimes stumble upon Carbink sleeping deep underground. The stone on top of its head can fire beams of energy.

TYPE:
ROCK-
FAIRY

Does not evolve

CHATOT
Music Note Pokémon

TYPE:
NORMAL-
FLYING

How to say it: CHAT-tot

Height: 1' 08"   **Weight:** 4.2 lbs.

Possible Moves: Hyper Voice, Chatter, Confide, Taunt, Peck, Growl, Mirror Move, Sing, Fury Attack, Round, Mimic, Echoed Voice, Roost, Uproar, Synchronoise, Feather Dance

Chatot can mimic other Pokémon's cries and even human speech. A group of them will often pick up the same phrase and keep repeating it among themselves.

Does not evolve

CHIMECHO
Wind Chime Pokémon

How to say it: chime-ECK-ko

Height: 2' 00"
Weight: 2.2 lbs.

Possible Moves: Healing Wish, Synchronoise, Wrap, Growl, Astonish, Confusion, Uproar, Take Down, Yawn, Psywave, Double-Edge, Heal Bell, Safeguard, Extrasensory, Heal Pulse

The top of Chimecho's head is a sucker that lets it hang from a ceiling or a tree branch. It's light enough to float on the wind.

TYPE:
PSYCHIC

Chingling → Chimecho

CHINCHOU
Angler Pokémon

How to say it: CHIN-chow

Height: 1' 08"   **Weight:** 26.5 lbs.

Possible Moves: Water Gun, Supersonic, Thunder Wave, Flail, Bubble, Confuse Ray, Spark, Take Down, Electro Ball, Bubble Beam, Signal Beam, Discharge, Aqua Ring, Hydro Pump, Ion Deluge, Charge

Chinchou live deep in the ocean, where they flash the lights on their antennae to communicate. They can also pass electricity between their antennae.

TYPE:
WATER-
ELECTRIC

Chinchou → Lanturn

CHINGLING
Bell Pokémon

How to say it: CHING-ling

Height: 0' 08"
Weight: 1.3 lbs.

Possible Moves: Wrap, Growl, Astonish, Confusion, Uproar, Last Resort, Entrainment

When Chingling hops about, a small orb bounces around inside its mouth, producing a noise like the sound of bells. It uses high-pitched sounds to attack its opponents' hearing.

TYPE:
PSYCHIC

Chingling   Chimecho

CLAMPERL
Bivalve Pokémon

How to say it: CLAM-perl

TYPE:
WATER

Height: 1' 04"
Weight: 115.7 lbs.

Possible Moves: Clamp, Water Gun, Whirlpool, Iron Defense, Shell Smash

The glorious pearl it produces can be used as a focus for mystical powers. Over its lifetime, a Clamperl will only create a single pearl.

Huntail

Clamperl   Gorebyss

CLAUNCHER

Water Gun Pokémon

How to say it: CLAWN-chur

Height: 1' 08"
Weight: 18.3 lbs.

Possible Moves: Splash, Water Gun, Water Sport, Vice Grip, Bubble, Flail, Bubble Beam, Swords Dance, Crabhammer, Water Pulse, Smack Down, Aqua Jet, Muddy Water

Clauncher shoots water from its claws with a force that can pulverize rock. Its range is great enough to knock flying Pokémon out of the air.

TYPE:
WATER

Clauncher → Clawitzer

CLAWITZER

Howitzer Pokémon

How to say it: CLOW-wit-zur

Height: 4' 03"
Weight: 77.8 lbs.

Possible Moves:
Heal Pulse, Dark Pulse, Dragon Pulse, Aura Sphere, Splash, Water Gun, Water Sport, Vice Grip, Bubble, Flail, Bubble Beam, Swords Dance, Crabhammer, Water Pulse, Smack Down, Aqua Jet, Muddy Water

Clawitzer's giant claw can expel massive jets of water at high speed. It fires the water forward to attack, or backward to propel itself through the sea.

TYPE:
WATER

Clauncher → Clawitzer

CLOYSTER
Bivalve Pokémon

How to say it: CLOY-stur

Height: 4' 11"
Weight: 292.1 lbs.

Possible Moves: Hydro Pump, Shell Smash, Toxic Spikes, Withdraw, Supersonic, Protect, Aurora Beam, Spike Cannon, Spikes, Icicle Crash

Cloyster with sharp spikes on their shells tend to live in a part of the sea where the current is particularly strong. They keep their shells closed except to attack.

TYPE:
WATER-ICE

Shellder ➡ Cloyster

CORSOLA
Coral Pokémon

How to say it: COR-soh-la

Height: 2' 00"
Weight: 11.0 lbs.

Possible Moves: Tackle, Harden, Bubble, Recover, Refresh, Bubble Beam, Ancient Power, Lucky Chant, Spike Cannon, Iron Defense, Rock Blast, Endure, Aqua Ring, Power Gem, Mirror Coat, Earth Power, Flail

Corsola is constantly shedding coral from its body as it grows. In polluted water, its branches become discolored.

TYPE:
WATER-ROCK

Does not evolve

CRUSTLE
Stone Home Pokémon

TYPE:
BUG-ROCK

How to say it: KRUS-tul

Height: 4' 07"
Weight: 440.9 lbs.

Possible Moves: Shell Smash, Rock Blast, Withdraw, Sand Attack, Feint Attack, Smack Down, Rock Polish, Bug Bite, Stealth Rock, Rock Slide, Slash, X-Scissor, Flail, Rock Wrecker

Because Crustle carries a heavy slab of rock everywhere it goes, its legs are extremely strong. Battles between them are determined by whose rock breaks first.

Dwebble   Crustle

CUBONE
Lonely Pokémon

TYPE: GROUND

How to say it: CUE-bone

Height: 1' 04" **Weight:** 14.3 lbs.

Possible Moves: Growl, Tail Whip, Bone Club, Headbutt, Leer, Focus Energy, Bonemerang, Rage, False Swipe, Thrash, Fling, Bone Rush, Endeavor, Double-Edge, Retaliate

Cubone wears its mother's skull as a helmet and always keeps its face hidden. When it's lonely, its cries become very loud.

Cubone   Marowak

DEDENNE

Antenna Pokémon

How to say it: deh-DEN-nay

Height: 0' 08"
Weight: 4.9 lbs.

TYPE:
ELECTRIC-
FAIRY

Possible Moves: Tackle, Tail Whip, Thunder Shock, Charge, Charm, Parabolic Charge, Nuzzle, Thunder Wave, Volt Switch, Rest, Snore, Charge Beam, Entrainment, Play Rough, Thunder, Discharge

Dedenne uses its whiskers like antennae to communicate over long distances using electrical waves. It can soak up electricity through its tail.

Does not evolve

DRAGALGE

Mock Kelp Pokémon

How to say it: druh-GAL-jee

Height: 5' 11"
Weight: 179.7 lbs.

TYPE:
POISON-
DRAGON

Possible Moves: Dragon Tail, Twister, Tackle, Smokescreen, Water Gun, Feint Attack, Tail Whip, Bubble, Acid, Camouflage, Poison Tail, Water Pulse, Double Team, Toxic, Aqua Tail, Sludge Bomb, Hydro Pump, Dragon Pulse

Toxic and territorial, Dragalge defend their homes from anything that enters. Even large ships aren't safe from their poison.

Skrelp ➡ **Dragalge**

DRIFBLIM

Blimp Pokémon

TYPE:
GHOST-
FLYING

How to say it: DRIFF-blim

Height: 3' 11"
Weight: 33.1 lbs.

Possible Moves: Phantom Force, Constrict, Minimize, Astonish, Gust, Focus Energy, Payback, Ominous Wind, Stockpile, Hex, Swallow, Spit Up, Shadow Ball, Amnesia, Baton Pass, Explosion

During the day, Drifblim tend to be sleepy. They take flight at dusk, but since they can't control their direction, they'll drift away wherever the wind blows them.

Drifloon   Drifblim

DRIFLOON

Balloon Pokémon

TYPE:
GHOST-
FLYING

How to say it: DRIFF-loon

Height: 1' 04"   **Weight:** 2.6 lbs.

Possible Moves: Constrict, Minimize, Astonish, Gust, Focus Energy, Payback, Ominous Wind, Stockpile, Hex, Swallow, Spit Up, Shadow Ball, Amnesia, Baton Pass, Explosion

Known as the "Signpost for Wandering Spirits," Drifloon itself was formed by spirits. It prefers humid weather and is happiest when it's floating through damp air.

Drifloon   Drifblim

DUOSION
Mitosis Pokémon

How to say it: doo-OH-zhun

Height: 2' 00"   **Weight:** 17.6 lbs.

Possible Moves: Psywave, Reflect, Rollout, Snatch, Hidden Power, Light Screen, Charm, Recover, Psyshock, Endeavor, Future Sight, Pain Split, Psychic, Skill Swap, Heal Block, Wonder Room

Duosion's brain is divided into two, so sometimes it tries to do two different things at the same time. When the brains are thinking together, Duosion's psychic power is at its strongest.

Solosis   Duosion   Reuniclus

DWEBBLE
Rock Inn Pokémon

How to say it: DWEHB-bul

Height: 1' 00"   **Weight:** 32.0 lbs.

Possible Moves: Fury Cutter, Rock Blast, Withdraw, Sand Attack, Feint Attack, Smack Down, Rock Polish, Bug Bite, Stealth Rock, Rock Slide, Slash, X-Scissor, Shell Smash, Flail, Rock Wrecker

Using a special liquid from its mouth, Dwebble hollows out a rock to use as its shell. It becomes very anxious without a proper rock.

Dwebble   Crustle

EEVEE
Evolution Pokémon

How to say it:
EE-vee

Height: 1' 00"
Weight: 14.3 lbs.

Possible Moves: Helping Hand, Growl, Tackle, Tail Whip, Sand Attack, Baby-Doll Eyes, Swift, Quick Attack, Bite, Refresh, Covet, Take Down, Charm, Baton Pass, Double-Edge, Last Resort, Trump Card

The amazingly adaptive Eevee can evolve into many different Pokémon, depending on its environment. This allows it to withstand harsh conditions.

TYPE:
NORMAL

Jolteon

Flareon

Glaceon

Vaporeon

Eevee

Espeon

Umbreon

Sylveon

Leafeon

ELECTRIKE
Lightning Pokémon

TYPE:
ELECTRIC

How to say it: eh-LEK-trike

Height: 2' 00"
Weight: 33.5 lbs.

Possible Moves: Tackle, Thunder Wave, Leer, Howl, Quick Attack, Spark, Odor Sleuth, Bite, Thunder Fang, Roar, Discharge, Charge, Wild Charge, Thunder

Electrike's fur soaks up static electricity. When a thunderstorm is coming, the electricity in the air makes it throw sparks.

Electrike   Manectric   Mega Manectric

EMOLGA
Sky Squirrel Pokémon

How to say it: ee-MAHL-guh

Height: 1' 04"   **Weight:** 11.0 lbs.

Possible Moves: Thunder Shock, Quick Attack, Tail Whip, Charge, Spark, Nuzzle, Pursuit, Double Team, Shock Wave, Electro Ball, Acrobatics, Light Screen, Encore, Volt Switch, Agility, Discharge

When Emolga stretches out its limbs, the membrane connecting them spreads like a cape and allows it to glide through the air. It makes its abode high in the trees.

TYPE:
ELECTRIC-
FLYING

Does not evolve

ESPEON

Sun Pokémon

How to say it: ESS-pee-on

Height: 2' 11"   **Weight:** 58.4 lbs.

Possible Moves: Helping Hand, Tackle, Tail Whip, Sand Attack, Confusion, Quick Attack, Swift, Psybeam, Future Sight, Psych Up, Morning Sun, Psychic, Last Resort, Power Swap

The incredibly sensitive fur covering Espeon's body can detect even the tiniest movement of the air. This allows it to sense changes in the weather and predict what its opponent will do next.

TYPE: PSYCHIC

Eevee   Espeon

EXEGGCUTE

Egg Pokémon

How to say it: ECKS-egg-cute

Height: 1' 04"   **Weight:** 5.5 lbs.

Possible Moves: Barrage, Uproar, Hypnosis, Reflect, Leech Seed, Bullet Seed, Stun Spore, Poison Powder, Sleep Powder, Confusion, Worry Seed, Natural Gift, Solar Beam, Extrasensory, Bestow

The six eggs that make up Exeggcute's body can be separated from one another, but thanks to their telepathic communication, they can find one another again quickly.

TYPE: GRASS-PSYCHIC

Exeggcute   Exeggutor

EXEGGUTOR

Coconut Pokémon

How to say it: eck-EGG-u-tore

Height: 6' 07"
Weight: 264.6 lbs.

Possible Moves: Seed Bomb, Barrage, Hypnosis, Confusion, Stomp, Psyshock, Egg Bomb, Wood Hammer, Leaf Storm

Although Exeggutor's three heads have minds of their own, they get along quite well. It's known as "The Walking Jungle."

TYPE:
GRASS-
PSYCHIC

Exeggcute   Exeggutor

FERROSEED

Thorn Seed Pokémon

TYPE:
GRASS-
STEEL

How to say it: fer-AH-seed

Height: 2' 00"   **Weight:** 41.4 lbs.

Possible Moves: Tackle, Harden, Rollout, Curse, Metal Claw, Pin Missile, Gyro Ball, Iron Defense, Mirror Shot, Ingrain, Self-Destruct, Iron Head, Payback, Flash Cannon, Explosion

Ferroseed use their spikes to cling to cave ceilings and absorb iron. They can also shoot those spikes to cover their escape when enemies approach.

Ferroseed   Ferrothorn

FERROTHORN

Thorn Pod Pokémon

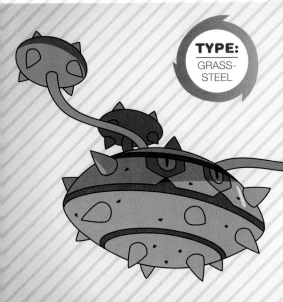

TYPE:
GRASS-STEEL

How to say it: fer-AH-thorn

Height: 3' 03"
Weight: 242.5 lbs.

Possible Moves: Rock Climb, Tackle, Harden, Rollout, Curse, Metal Claw, Pin Missile, Gyro Ball, Iron Defense, Mirror Shot, Ingrain, Self-Destruct, Power Whip, Iron Head, Payback, Flash Cannon, Explosion

Ferrothorn swings its spiked feelers to attack. It likes to hang from the ceiling of a cave and shower spikes on anyone passing below.

Ferroseed   Ferrothorn

FLAAFFY

Wool Pokémon

TYPE:
ELECTRIC

How to say it: FLAH-fee

Height: 2' 07" **Weight:** 29.3 lbs.

Possible Moves: Tackle, Growl, Thunder Wave, Thunder Shock, Cotton Spore, Charge, Take Down, Electro Ball, Confuse Ray, Power Gem, Discharge, Cotton Guard, Signal Beam, Light Screen, Thunder

Though Flaaffy's fluffy coat attracts electricity, it never has to worry about getting shocked, because its body is protected by rubbery skin. Its tail lights up when it's fully charged.

Mareep   Flaaffy   Ampharos   Mega Ampha

FLAREON
Flame Pokémon

How to say it: FLAIR-ee-on

Height: 2' 11"
Weight: 55.1 lbs.

TYPE:
FIRE

Possible Moves: Helping Hand, Tackle, Tail Whip, Sand Attack, Ember, Quick Attack, Bite, Fire Fang, Fire Spin, Scary Face, Smog, Lava Plume, Last Resort, Flare Blitz

The flame sac inside Flareon's body powers its intense fiery breath. When it's preparing for battle, its body temperature can reach more than 1,500 degrees Fahrenheit.

Eevee → Flareon

GIGALITH
Compressed Pokémon

How to say it: GIH-gah-lith

Height: 5' 07"   **Weight:** 573.2 lbs.

TYPE:
ROCK

Possible Moves: Tackle, Harden, Sand Attack, Headbutt, Rock Blast, Mud-Slap, Iron Defense, Smack Down, Power Gem, Rock Slide, Stealth Rock, Sandstorm, Stone Edge, Explosion

After Gigalith soaks up the sun's rays, it uses its energy core to process that energy into a weapon. A blast of its compressed energy can destroy a mountain.

Roggenrola → Boldore → Gigalith

GLACEON
Fresh Snow Pokémon

TYPE:
ICE

How to say it: GLACE-ee-on

Height: 2' 07"
Weight: 57.1 lbs.

Possible Moves: Helping Hand, Tackle, Tail Whip, Sand Attack, Icy Wind, Quick Attack, Bite, Ice Fang, Ice Shard, Barrier, Mirror Coat, Hail, Last Resort, Blizzard

The icy Glaceon has amazing control over its body temperature. It can freeze its own fur and then fire the frozen hairs like needles at an opponent.

Eevee → Glaceon

GOLETT
Automaton Pokémon

TYPE:
GROUND-GHOST

How to say it: GO-let

Height: 3' 03"
Weight: 202.8 lbs.

Possible Moves: Pound, Astonish, Defense Curl, Mud-Slap, Rollout, Shadow Punch, Iron Defense, Mega Punch, Magnitude, Dynamic Punch, Night Shade, Curse, Earthquake, Hammer Arm, Focus Punch

Sculpted from clay and animated by a mysterious internal energy, Golett are the product of ancient science.

Golett → Golurk

GOLURK

Automaton Pokémon

How to say it: GO-lurk

Height: 9' 02"
Weight: 727.5 lbs.

Possible Moves: Phantom Force, Focus Punch, Pound, Astonish, Defense Curl, Mud-Slap, Rollout, Shadow Punch, Iron Defense, Mega Punch, Magnitude, Dynamic Punch, Night Shade, Curse, Heavy Slam, Earthquake, Hammer Arm

The seal on Golurk's chest keeps its energy contained and stops it from going wild. Long ago, these Pokémon were created as protectors.

Golett → Golurk

TYPE:
GROUND-GHOST

GOREBYSS

South Sea Pokémon

TYPE:
WATER

How to say it: GORE-a-biss

Height: 5' 11"
Weight: 49.8 lbs.

Possible Moves: Whirlpool, Confusion, Agility, Water Pulse, Amnesia, Aqua Ring, Captivate, Baton Pass, Dive, Psychic, Aqua Tail, Hydro Pump

Gorebyss heralds the arrival of spring by turning even more vividly pink. Its long, thin mouth can reach into crevices in the rocky seafloor to eat the seaweed that grows there.

Clamperl → Gorebyss

GRANBULL
Fairy Pokémon

How to say it: GRAN-bull

TYPE:
FAIRY

Height: 4' 07"
Weight: 107.4 lbs.

Possible Moves: Outrage, Ice Fang, Fire Fang, Thunder Fang, Tackle, Scary Face, Tail Whip, Charm, Bite, Lick, Headbutt, Roar, Rage, Play Rough, Payback, Crunch

With its giant fangs and gaping mouth, Granbull looks scary, but it's actually very timid. Its best bet in battle is to frighten an opponent into running away.

Snubbull Granbull

GRUMPIG
Manipulate Pokémon

How to say it: GRUM-pig

Height: 2' 11"
Weight: 157.6 lbs.

TYPE:
PSYCHIC

Possible Moves: Splash, Psywave, Psybeam, Odor Sleuth, Psych Up, Confuse Ray, Magic Coat, Zen Headbutt, Rest, Snore, Power Gem, Psyshock, Payback, Psychic, Bounce

When Grumpig does an odd little dance, it's trying to use mind control on its opponents. The black pearls on its body boost its mystical powers.

Spoink Grumpig

HARIYAMA

Arm Thrust Pokémon

TYPE:
FIGHTING

How to say it: HAR-ee-YAH-mah

Height: 7' 07" **Weight:** 559.5 lbs.

Possible Moves: Brine, Tackle, Focus Energy, Sand Attack, Arm Thrust, Vital Throw, Fake Out, Whirlwind, Knock Off, Smelling Salts, Belly Drum, Force Palm, Seismic Toss, Wake-Up Slap, Endure, Close Combat, Reversal, Heavy Slam

Hariyama's arms are so strong that a single punch can send a heavy truck flying through the air. It challenges bigger Pokémon to tests of strength.

Makuhita   Hariyama

HAWLUCHA

Wrestling Pokémon

How to say it: haw-LOO-cha

Height: 2' 07"
Weight: 47.4 lbs.

Possible Moves: Detect, Tackle, Hone Claws, Karate Chop, Wing Attack, Roost, Aerial Ace, Encore, Fling, Flying Press, Bounce, Endeavor, Feather Dance, High Jump Kick, Sky Attack, Sky Drop, Swords Dance

Hawlucha prefers to fight by diving at its foes from above. This aerial advantage makes up for its small size.

TYPE:
FIGHTING-
FLYING

Does not evolve

HELIOLISK
Generator Pokémon

TYPE:
ELECTRIC-
NORMAL

How to say it: HEE-lee-oh-lisk

Height: 3' 03"
Weight: 46.3 lbs.

Possible Moves: Eerie Impulse,
Electrify, Razor Wind, Quick Attack,
Thunder, Charge, Parabolic Charge

Heliolisk generates electricity by
spreading its frill out wide to soak up
the sun. It uses this energy to boost
its speed.

Helioptile   Heliolisk

HELIOPTILE
Generator Pokémon

TYPE:
ELECTRIC-
NORMAL

How to say it: hee-lee-AHP-tile

Height: 1' 08"
Weight: 13.2 lbs.

Possible Moves: Pound, Tail
Whip, Thunder Shock, Charge,
Mud-Slap, Quick Attack, Razor
Wind, Parabolic Charge, Thunder
Wave, Bulldoze, Volt Switch,
Electrify, Thunderbolt

The frills on Helioptile's head soak
up sunlight and create electricity.
In this way, they can generate
enough energy to keep them
going without food.

Helioptile   Heliolisk

HERACROSS

Single Horn Pokémon

TYPE:
BUG-
FIGHTING

How to say it: HAIR-uh-cross

Height: 4' 11"
Weight: 119.0 lbs.

Possible Moves: Arm Thrust, Bullet Seed, Night Slash, Tackle, Leer, Horn Attack, Endure, Fury Attack, Aerial Ace, Chip Away, Counter, Brick Break, Take Down, Pin Missile, Close Combat, Feint, Reversal, Megahorn

Heracross is immensely strong. With its giant horn, it can throw an enemy much bigger than itself.

MEGA HERACROSS

Single Horn Pokémon

Height: 5' 07"
Weight: 137.8 lbs.

TYPE:
BUG-
FIGHTING

Heracross   Mega Heracross

HIPPOPOTAS
Hippo Pokémon

TYPE: GROUND

How to say it: HIP-poh-puh-TOSS

Height: 2' 07"
Weight: 109.1 lbs.

Possible Moves: Tackle, Sand Attack, Bite, Yawn, Take Down, Dig, Sand Tomb, Crunch, Earthquake, Double-Edge, Fissure

Hippopotas lives in a dry environment. Its body gives off sand instead of sweat, and this sandy shield keeps it protected from water and germs.

Hippopotas   Hippowdon

HIPPOWDON
Heavyweight Pokémon

TYPE: GROUND

How to say it: hip-POW-don

Height: 6' 07"
Weight: 661.4 lbs.

Possible Moves: Ice Fang, Fire Fang, Thunder Fang, Tackle, Sand Attack, Bite, Yawn, Take Down, Dig, Sand Tomb, Crunch, Earthquake, Double-Edge, Fissure

Hippowdon stores sand inside its body and expels it through the ports on its sides to create a twisting sandstorm in battle.

Hippopotas   Hippowdon

HORSEA
Dragon Pokémon

How to say it: HOR-see

Height: 1' 04" **Weight:** 17.6 lbs.

Possible Moves: Water Gun, Smokescreen, Leer, Bubble, Focus Energy, Bubble Beam, Agility, Twister, Brine, Hydro Pump, Dragon Dance, Dragon Pulse

When threatened, Horsea covers its retreat by spitting a murky cloud of ink. It prefers to nest in coral.

TYPE:
WATER

Horsea   Seadra   Kingdra

HOUNDOOM

Dark Pokémon

How to say it: HOWN-doom

Height: 4' 07"
Weight: 77.2 lbs.

Possible Moves: Inferno, Nasty Plot, Thunder Fang, Leer, Ember, Howl, Smog, Roar, Bite, Odor Sleuth, Beat Up, Fire Fang, Feint Attack, Embargo, Foul Play, Flamethrower, Crunch

Houndoom's eerie howl was once thought to be a bad omen. Its fiery breath causes a painful burn that never heals.

TYPE:
DARK-
FIRE

MEGA HOUNDOOM

Dark Pokémon

Height: 6' 03"
Weight: 109.1 lbs.

TYPE:
DARK-
FIRE

Houndour ➡ Houndoom ➡ Mega Houndoom

HOUNDOUR
Dark Pokémon

TYPE:
DARK-FIRE

How to say it: HOWN-dowr

Height: 2' 00"
Weight: 23.8 lbs.

Possible Moves: Leer, Ember, Howl, Smog, Roar, Bite, Odor Sleuth, Beat Up, Fire Fang, Feint Attack, Embargo, Foul Play, Flamethrower, Crunch, Nasty Plot, Inferno

If you hear a spine-chilling howl just at sunrise, you might have wandered into Houndour's territory.

oundour   Houndoom   Mega Houndoom

HUNTAIL
Deep Sea Pokémon

TYPE:
WATER

How to say it: HUN-tail

Height: 5' 07"
Weight: 59.5 lbs.

Possible Moves: Whirlpool, Bite, Screech, Water Pulse, Scary Face, Ice Fang, Brine, Baton Pass, Dive, Crunch, Aqua Tail, Hydro Pump

Huntail lives in the depths of the ocean, where it's always dark. Its lighted tail, which resembles a small creature, sometimes tricks others into attacking.

Clamperl   Huntail

INKAY
Revolving Pokémon

TYPE:
DARK-PSYCHIC

How to say it: in-kay

Height: 1' 04"   **Weight:** 7.7 lbs.

Possible Moves: Tackle, Peck, Constrict, Reflect, Foul Play, Swagger, Psywave, Topsy-Turvy, Hypnosis, Psybeam, Switcheroo, Payback, Light Screen, Pluck, Psycho Cut, Slash, Night Slash, Superpower

The spots on Inkay's body emit a flashing light. This light confuses its opponents, giving it a chance to escape.

Inkay   Malamar

JOLTEON
Lightning Pokémon

TYPE:
ELECTRIC

How to say it: JOL-tee-on

Height: 2' 07"   **Weight:** 54.0 lbs.

Possible Moves: Helping Hand, Tackle, Tail Whip, Sand Attack, Thunder Shock, Quick Attack, Double Kick, Thunder Fang, Pin Missile, Agility, Thunder Wave, Discharge, Last Resort, Thunder

When Jolteon's fur sticks straight out, it's building up an electric charge. It can gather electricity from the air around it to power its high-voltage attacks.

Eevee   Jolteon

KANGASKHAN

Parent Pokémon

TYPE:
NORMAL

How to say it: KANG-gas-con

Height: 7' 03"
Weight: 176.4 lbs.

Possible Moves: Comet Punch, Leer, Fake Out, Tail Whip, Bite, Double Hit, Rage, Mega Punch, Chip Away, Dizzy Punch, Crunch, Endure, Outrage, Sucker Punch, Reversal

The little one leaves the belly pouch only when it's safe to play outside. While it's out, Kangaskhan keeps careful watch.

MEGA KANGASKHAN

Parent Pokémon

Height: 7' 03"
Weight: 220.5 lbs.

TYPE:
NORMAL

Kangaskhan → Mega Kangaskhan

KINGDRA
Dragon Pokémon

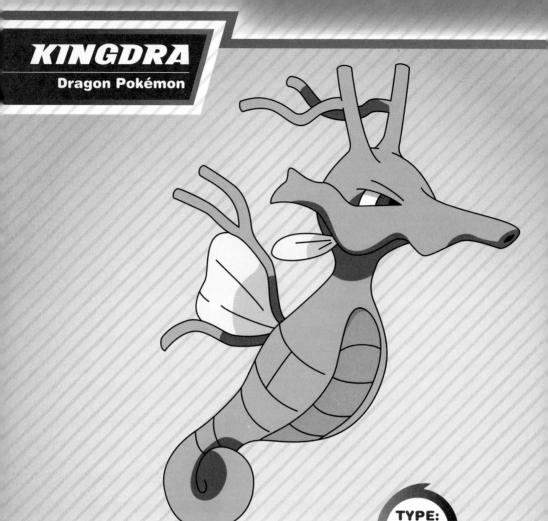

TYPE:
WATER-DRAGON

How to say it: KING-dra

Height: 5' 11"   **Weight:** 335.1 lbs.

Possible Moves: Dragon Pulse, Yawn, Water Gun, Smokescreen, Leer, Bubble, Focus Energy, Bubble Beam, Agility, Twister, Brine, Hydro Pump, Dragon Dance

Kingdra lives quite comfortably in the crushing depths of the ocean. When it yawns, it sucks in so much water that a whirlpool forms on the surface.

Horsea   Seadra   Kingdra

KROKOROK
Desert Croc Pokémon

TYPE:
GROUND-DARK

How to say it: KRAHK-oh-rahk

Height: 3' 03"
Weight: 73.6 lbs.

Possible Moves: Leer, Rage, Bite, Sand Attack, Torment, Sand Tomb, Assurance, Mud-Slap, Embargo, Swagger, Crunch, Dig, Scary Face, Foul Play, Sandstorm, Earthquake, Thrash

The membranes that cover Krokorok's eyes not only protect them during sandstorms, but also act like heat sensors, enabling it to navigate in total darkness.

Sandile   Krokorok   Krookodile

KROOKODILE
Intimidation Pokémon

TYPE:
GROUND-DARK

How to say it: KROOK-oh-dyle

Height: 4' 11"
Weight: 212.3 lbs.

Possible Moves: Outrage, Leer, Rage, Bite, Sand Attack, Torment, Sand Tomb, Assurance, Mud-Slap, Embargo, Swagger, Crunch, Dig, Scary Face, Foul Play, Sandstorm, Earthquake

Krookodile's formidable jaws are capable of crunching up cars. Triggered into violence by nearby movement, Krookodile will clamp onto its prey with all the might of those jaws.

Sandile   Krokorok   Krookodile

LANTURN
Light Pokémon

How to say it: LAN-turn

Height: 3' 11"
Weight: 49.6 lbs.

Possible Moves: Eerie Impulse, Water Gun, Supersonic, Thunder Wave, Flail, Bubble, Confuse Ray, Spark, Take Down, Stockpile, Swallow, Spit Up, Electro Ball, Bubble Beam, Signal Beam, Discharge, Aqua Ring, Hydro Pump, Ion Deluge, Charge

Even in the dark depths of the ocean, Lanturn's light can be seen from a great distance. Because of this, it's known as "The Deep-Sea Star."

Chinchou   Lanturn

LAPRAS
Transport Pokémon

TYPE: WATER-ICE

How to say it: LAP-rus

Height: 8' 02"   **Weight:** 485.0 lbs.

Possible Moves: Sing, Growl, Water Gun, Mist, Confuse Ray, Ice Shard, Water Pulse, Body Slam, Rain Dance, Perish Song, Ice Beam, Brine, Safeguard, Hydro Pump, Sheer Cold

Gentle and intelligent, Lapras are happy to carry travelers across the water on their sturdy backs. Because they are easily caught, wild Lapras are growing rarer.

Does not evolve

LEAFEON
Verdant Pokémon

TYPE:
GRASS

How to say it: LEAF-ee-on

Height: 3' 03"   **Weight:** 56.2 lbs.

Possible Moves: Tail Whip, Tackle, Helping Hand, Sand Attack, Razor Leaf, Quick Attack, Grass Whistle, Magical Leaf, Giga Drain, Swords Dance, Synthesis, Sunny Day, Last Resort, Leaf Blade

When Leafeon soaks up the sun for use in photosynthesis, it gives off clean, fresh air. It often takes naps in a sunny area to gather energy.

Eevee   Leafeon

LUNATONE
Meteorite Pokémon

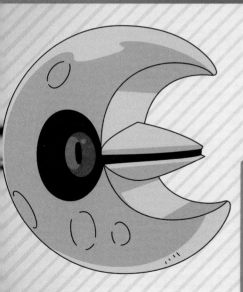

TYPE:
ROCK-
PSYCHIC

How to say it: LOO-nuh-tone

Height: 3' 03"   **Weight:** 370.4 lbs.

Possible Moves: Magic Room, Rock Throw, Tackle, Harden, Confusion, Hypnosis, Rock Polish, Psywave, Embargo, Rock Slide, Cosmic Power, Psychic, Heal Block, Stone Edge, Future Sight, Explosion, Moonblast

Lunatone can make its opponents sleep merely by staring at them. It's most active when the moon is full.

Does not evolve

LUVDISC

Rendezvous Pokémon

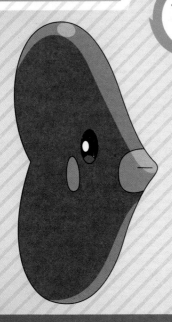

TYPE:
WATER

How to say it: LOVE-disk

Height: 2' 00"   **Weight:** 19.2 lbs.

Possible Moves: Tackle, Charm, Water Gun, Agility, Take Down, Lucky Chant, Water Pulse, Attract, Flail, Sweet Kiss, Hydro Pump, Aqua Ring, Captivate, Safeguard

During certain times of the year, so many Luvdisc gather around a single reef that the water appears to turn pink. They are rumored to bring endless love to couples that find them.

Does not evolve

MACHAMP

Superpower Pokémon

TYPE:
FIGHTING

How to say it: muh-CHAMP

Height: 5' 03"   **Weight:** 286.6 lbs.

Possible Moves: Wide Guard, Low Kick, Leer, Focus Energy, Karate Chop, Low Sweep, Foresight, Seismic Toss, Revenge, Vital Throw, Submission, Wake-Up Slap, Cross Chop, Scary Face, Dynamic Punch

With its four muscular arms, Machamp can unleash hundreds of punches a second or pin its opponent to the ground.

Machop   Machoke   Machamp

MACHOKE
Superpower Pokémon

TYPE:
FIGHTING

How to say it: muh-CHOKE

Height: 4' 11"
Weight: 155.4 lbs.

Possible Moves: Low Kick, Leer, Focus Energy, Karate Chop, Low Sweep, Foresight, Seismic Toss, Revenge, Vital Throw, Submission, Wake-Up Slap, Cross Chop, Scary Face, Dynamic Punch

Machoke is strong enough to pick up a dump truck with one arm. It channels this strength in a helpful way, often assisting people with heavy things.

Machop   Machoke   Machamp

MACHOP
Superpower Pokémon

TYPE:
FIGHTING

How to say it: muh-CHOP

Height: 2' 07"   **Weight:** 43.0 lbs.

Possible Moves: Low Kick, Leer, Focus Energy, Karate Chop, Low Sweep, Foresight, Seismic Toss, Revenge, Vital Throw, Submission, Wake-Up Slap, Cross Chop, Scary Face, Dynamic Punch

Machop lifts a Graveler like a weight to make its muscles stronger. It can throw opponents much bigger than itself.

Machop   Machoke   Machamp

MAKUHITA

Guts Pokémon

How to say it: MAK-oo-HEE-ta

Height: 3' 03"   **Weight:** 190.5 lbs.

Possible Moves: Tackle, Focus Energy, Sand Attack, Arm Thrust, Vital Throw, Fake Out, Whirlwind, Knock Off, Smelling Salts, Belly Drum, Force Palm, Seismic Toss, Wake-Up Slap, Endure, Close Combat, Reversal, Heavy Slam

By repeatedly slamming its body into sturdy tree trunks, Makuhita toughens itself up for battle. Its severe training gives it a fierce fighting spirit.

Makuhita   Hariyama

MALAMAR

Overturning Pokémon

How to say it: MAL-uh-MAR

Height: 4' 11"   **Weight:** 103.6 lbs.

Possible Moves: Superpower, Reversal, Tackle, Peck, Constrict, Reflect, Foul Play, Swagger, Psywave, Topsy-Turvy, Hypnosis, Psybeam, Switcheroo, Payback, Light Screen, Pluck, Psycho Cut, Slash, Night Slash

With hypnotic compulsion, Malamar can control the actions of others, forcing them to do its will. The movement of its tentacles can put anyone watching into a trance.

Inkay   Malamar

MANECTRIC

Discharge Pokémon

TYPE:
ELECTRIC

How to say it: mane-EK-trick

Height: 4' 11"
Weight: 88.6 lbs.

Possible Moves: Electric Terrain, Fire Fang, Tackle, Thunder Wave, Leer, Howl, Quick Attack, Spark, Odor Sleuth, Bite, Thunder Fang, Roar, Discharge, Charge, Wild Charge, Thunder

In places where lightning strikes the ground, Manectric makes its nest. Its mane gives off an electric charge.

MEGA MANECTRIC

Discharge Pokémon

Height: 5' 11"
Weight: 97.0 lbs.

TYPE:
ELECTRIC

Electrike   Manectric   Mega Manectric

MANTINE

Kite Pokémon

How to say it: MAN-tine

Height: 6' 11"
Weight: 485.0 lbs.

Possible Moves:
Psybeam, Bullet Seed, Signal Beam, Tackle, Bubble, Supersonic, Bubble Beam, Confuse Ray, Wing Attack, Headbutt, Water Pulse, Wide Guard, Take Down, Agility, Air Slash, Aqua Ring, Bounce, Hydro Pump

An elegant and speedy swimmer, Mantine can gain enough momentum to launch itself out of the water and fly for hundreds of feet before splashing down again.

TYPE:
WATER-
FLYING

Mantyke   Mantine

MANTYKE

Kite Pokémon

TYPE:
WATER-
FLYING

How to say it: MAN-tike

Height: 3' 03"
Weight: 143.3 lbs.

Possible Moves: Tackle, Bubble, Supersonic, Bubble Beam, Confuse Ray, Wing Attack, Headbutt, Water Pulse, Wide Guard, Take Down, Agility, Air Slash, Aqua Ring, Bounce, Hydro Pump

Mantyke that live in different regions have different patterns on their backs. They're often found in the company of Remoraid.

Mantyke   Mantine

MAREEP
Wool Pokémon

How to say it: mah-REEP

TYPE: ELECTRIC

Height: 2' 00"
Weight: 17.2 lbs.

Possible Moves: Tackle, Growl, Thunder Wave, Thunder Shock, Cotton Spore, Charge, Take Down, Electro Ball, Confuse Ray, Power Gem, Discharge, Cotton Guard, Signal Beam, Light Screen, Thunder

When static electricity builds up in Mareep's body, its soft coat puffs up to double its usual size. The fluffy wool helps regulate its temperature.

Mareep   Flaaffy   Ampharos   Mega Ampharos

MAROWAK
Bone Keeper Pokémon

TYPE: GROUND

How to say it: MAR-oh-wack

Height: 3' 03"   **Weight:** 99.2 lbs.

Possible Moves: Growl, Tail Whip, Bone Club, Headbutt, Leer, Focus Energy, Bonemerang, Rage, False Swipe, Thrash, Fling, Bone Rush, Endeavor, Double-Edge, Retaliate

Using bones as weapons has given Marowak a fierce temperament. It can knock out an opponent with a skillfully thrown bone.

Cubone   Marowak

MAWILE
Deceiver Pokémon

How to say it: MAW-while

Height: 2' 00"
Weight: 25.4 lbs.

Possible Moves:
Play Rough, Iron Head, Taunt, Growl, Fairy Wind, Astonish, Fake Tears, Bite, Sweet Scent, Vice Grip, Feint Attack, Baton Pass, Crunch, Iron Defense, Sucker Punch, Stockpile, Swallow, Spit Up

The massive jaws on the back of Mawile's head are strong enough to crunch up iron beams.

TYPE:
STEEL-FAIRY

MEGA MAWILE
Deceiver Pokémon

Height: 3' 03"
Weight: 51.8 lbs.

TYPE:
STEEL-FAIRY

Mawile → Mega Mawile

MIENFOO
Martial Arts Pokémon

How to say it: MEEN-FOO

TYPE: FIGHTING

Height: 2' 11"
Weight: 44.1 lbs.

Possible Moves: Pound, Meditate, Detect, Fake Out, Double Slap, Swift, Calm Mind, Force Palm, Drain Punch, Jump Kick, U-turn, Quick Guard, Bounce, High Jump Kick, Reversal, Aura Sphere

In battle, Mienfoo never stops moving, flowing through one attack after another with grace and speed. Its claws are very sharp.

Mienfoo → Mienshao

MIENSHAO
Martial Arts Pokémon

TYPE: FIGHTING

How to say it: MEEN-SHOW

Height: 4' 07"   **Weight:** 78.3 lbs.

Possible Moves: Aura Sphere, Reversal, Pound, Meditate, Detect, Fake Out, Double Slap, Swift, Calm Mind, Force Palm, Drain Punch, Jump Kick, U-turn, Wide Guard, Bounce, High Jump Kick

With the long, whiplike fur on its arms, Mienshao can unleash a flurry of attacks so fast they're almost invisible. Its battle combos are unstoppable.

Mienfoo → Mienshao

MILTANK
Milk Cow Pokémon

How to say it: MILL-tank

Height: 3' 11"   **Weight:** 166.4 lbs.

Possible Moves: Tackle, Growl, Defense Curl, Stomp, Milk Drink, Bide, Rollout, Body Slam, Zen Headbutt, Captivate, Gyro Ball, Heal Bell, Wake-Up Slap

When Miltank spends time with babies, its milk becomes even more nourishing. Those who are ill or tired consume this nutritious milk to feel better.

Does not evolve

MIME JR.
Mime Pokémon

TYPE: PSYCHIC-FAIRY

How to say it: mime JOO-nyur

Height: 2' 00"   **Weight:** 28.7 lbs.

Possible Moves: Tickle, Barrier, Confusion, Copycat, Meditate, Double Slap, Mimic, Encore, Light Screen, Reflect, Psybeam, Substitute, Recycle, Trick, Psychic, Role Play, Baton Pass, Safeguard

To enthrall and confuse an attacker, Mime Jr. copies its movements. While the opponent is bewildered, it makes its escape.

Mime Jr.   Mr. Mime

LEGENDARY POKÉMON

MOLTRES
Flame Pokémon

TYPE: FIRE-FLYING

How to say it: MOL-trays

Height: 6' 07"
Weight: 132.3 lbs.

Possible Moves: Roost, Hurricane, Sky Attack, Heat Wave, Wing Attack, Ember, Fire Spin, Agility, Endure, Ancient Power, Flamethrower, Safeguard, Air Slash, Sunny Day, Solar Beam

It is said that when Moltres appears, spring is not far behind. This Legendary Pokémon gives off flames as it flaps its wings.

Does not evolve

MR. MIME
Barrier Pokémon

TYPE: PSYCHIC-FAIRY

How to say it: MIS-ter MIME

Height: 4' 03"
Weight: 120.1 lbs.

Possible Moves: Misty Terrain, Magical Leaf, Quick Guard, Wide Guard, Power Swap, Guard Swap, Barrier, Confusion, Copycat, Meditate, Double Slap, Mimic, Psywave, Encore, Light Screen, Reflect, Psybeam, Substitute, Recycle, Trick, Psychic, Role Play, Baton Pass, Safeguard

When it mimes being stuck behind an invisible wall, Mr. Mime is actually creating a psychic barrier with its fingertips. This barrier protects it from attacks.

Mime Jr.   Mr. Mime

NIDOKING

Drill Pokémon

TYPE:
POISON-
GROUND

How to say it: NEE-doe-king

Height: 4' 07"
Weight: 136.7 lbs.

Possible Moves: Megahorn, Peck, Focus Energy, Double Kick, Poison Sting, Chip Away, Thrash, Earth Power

Nidoking's hide is as hard as stone, and its tail is strong enough to snap a tree trunk effortlessly. In addition, the long horn on its head is full of venom. Stay clear!

Nidoran♂ → Nidorino → Nidoking

NIDOQUEEN

Drill Pokémon

How to say it: NEE-doe-kween

Height: 4' 03"   **Weight:** 132.3 lbs.

Possible Moves: Superpower, Scratch, Tail Whip, Double Kick, Poison Sting, Chip Away, Body Slam, Earth Power

Stiff scales like needles cover Nidoqueen's body. When guarding its nest, it can bristle up the scales so the needles point out toward any intruder.

TYPE:
POISON-
GROUND

Nidoran♀ → Nidorina → Nidoqueen

NIDORAN ♀

Poison Pin Pokémon

TYPE:
POISON

How to say it: : NEE-doe-ran

Height: 1' 04"
Weight: 15.4 lbs.

Possible Moves: Growl, Scratch, Tail Whip, Double Kick, Poison Sting, Fury Swipes, Bite, Helping Hand, Toxic Spikes, Flatter, Crunch, Captivate, Poison Fang

Nidoran ♀ is little and doesn't like to fight, but it should not be underestimated. Its body is covered in poisonous barbs, and the small horn on its forehead is toxic.

Nidoran ♀ ➡ Nidorina ➡ Nidoqueen

NIDORAN ♂

Poison Pin Pokémon

TYPE:
POISON

How to say it: NEE-doe-ran

Height: 1' 04"   **Weight:** 15.4 lbs.

Possible Moves: Leer, Peck, Focus Energy, Double Kick, Poison Sting, Fury Attack, Horn Attack, Helping Hand, Toxic Spikes, Flatter, Poison Jab, Captivate, Horn Drill

When Nidoran ♂ lifts its large ears above the grass, it's listening for anything that could be a threat. Its poison barbs can be extended for protection.

Nidoran ♂ ➡ Nidorino ➡ Nidoking

NIDORINA
Poison Pin Pokémon

TYPE:
POISON

How to say it: NEE-doe-REE-na

Height: 2' 07"   **Weight:** 44.1 lbs.

Possible Moves: Growl, Scratch, Tail Whip, Double Kick, Poison Sting, Fury Swipes, Bite, Helping Hand, Toxic Spikes, Flatter, Crunch, Captivate, Poison Fang

The gentle Nidorina protects itself with cries containing ultrasonic waves that confuse and bewilder attackers.

Nidoran ♀   Nidorina   Nidoqueen

NIDORINO
Poison Pin Pokémon

TYPE:
POISON

How to say it: NEE-doe-REE-no

Height: 2' 11"   **Weight:** 43.0 lbs.

Possible Moves: Leer, Peck, Focus Energy, Double Kick, Poison Sting, Fury Attack, Horn Attack, Helping Hand, Toxic Spikes, Flatter, Poison Jab, Captivate, Horn Drill

The aggressive Nidorino attacks without warning if it senses something amiss in its surroundings. The horn on its forehead is extremely poisonous.

Nidoran ♂   Nidorino   Nidoking

NOSEPASS

Compass Pokémon

TYPE: ROCK

How to say it: NOSE-pass

Height: 3' 03"   **Weight:** 213.8 lbs.

Possible Moves: Tackle, Harden, Block, Rock Throw, Thunder Wave, Rock Blast, Rest, Spark, Rock Slide, Power Gem, Sandstorm, Discharge, Earth Power, Stone Edge, Lock-On, Zap Cannon

Because its nose is magnetic, Nosepass always faces north, so travelers check it like a compass. Its nose sometimes attracts metal objects that it can use as a shield.

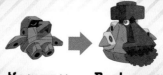

Nosepass   Probopass

OCTILLERY

Jet Pokémon

How to say it: ock-TILL-er-ree

Height: 2' 11"
Weight: 62.8 lbs.

TYPE:
WATER

Possible Moves: Gunk Shot, Rock Blast, Water Gun, Constrict, Psybeam, Aurora Beam, Bubble Beam, Focus Energy, Octazooka, Wring Out, Signal Beam, Ice Beam, Bullet Seed, Hydro Pump, Hyper Beam, Soak

Octillery doesn't like being out in the open. It hides itself among craggy rocks, where it can spray ink to keep enemies away without revealing itself.

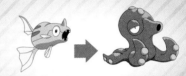

Remoraid → Octillery

ONIX

Rock Snake Pokémon

TYPE:
ROCK-
GROUND

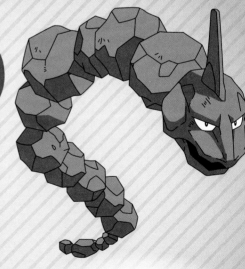

How to say it: ON-icks

Height: 28' 10"   **Weight:** 463.0 lbs.

Possible Moves: Mud Sport, Tackle, Harden, Bind, Curse, Rock Throw, Rock Tomb, Rage, Stealth Rock, Rock Polish, Gyro Ball, Smack Down, Dragon Breath, Slam, Screech, Rock Slide, Sand Tomb, Iron Tail, Dig, Stone Edge, Double-Edge, Sandstorm

When Onix is searching for food underground, it can bore through the soil at impressive speeds. Diglett sometimes live in the burrows it leaves behind.

Onix → Steelix

PACHIRISU

EleSquirrel Pokémon

How to say it: patch-ee-REE-sue

Height: 1' 04"   **Weight:** 8.6 lbs.

Possible Moves: Growl, Bide, Quick Attack, Charm, Spark, Endure, Nuzzle, Swift, Electro Ball, Sweet Kiss, Thunder Wave, Super Fang, Discharge, Last Resort, Hyper Fang

When Pachirisu affectionately rub their cheeks together, they're sharing electric energy with one another. The balls of fur they shed crackle with static.

TYPE:
ELECTRIC

Does not evolve

PELIPPER

Water Bird Pokémon

How to say it: PEL-ip-purr

Height: 3' 11"   **Weight:** 61.7 lbs.

Possible Moves: Hydro Pump, Tailwind, Soak, Growl, Water Gun, Water Sport, Wing Attack, Supersonic, Mist, Water Pulse, Payback, Protect, Roost, Brine, Stockpile, Swallow, Spit Up, Fling, Hurricane

With its enormous bill, Pelipper can scoop up large quantities of water and food from the sea. It's also been known to rescue small Pokémon from danger by carrying them in its bill.

TYPE:
WATER-
FLYING

Wingull   Pelipper

PINSIR
Stag Beetle Pokémon

How to say it: PIN-sir

Height: 4' 11"
Weight: 121.3 lbs.

Possible Moves: Vice Grip, Focus Energy, Bind, Seismic Toss, Harden, Revenge, Brick Break, Vital Throw, Submission, X-Scissor, Storm Throw, Thrash, Swords Dance, Superpower, Guillotine

Pinsir uses its long horns for both offense and defense. When it swings its head, the horns keep enemies at bay.

TYPE:
BUG

MEGA PINSIR
Stag Beetle Pokémon

Height: 5' 07"
Weight: 130.1 lbs.

TYPE:
BUG-
FLYING

Pinsir ➡ Mega Pinsir

PROBOPASS

Compass Pokémon

How to say it: PRO-bow-pass

Height: 4' 07"   **Weight:** 749.6 lbs.

Possible Moves: Magnet Rise, Gravity, Tackle, Iron Defense, Block, Magnet Bomb, Thunder Wave, Rock Blast, Rest, Spark, Rock Slide, Power Gem, Sandstorm, Discharge, Earth Power, Stone Edge, Lock-On, Zap Cannon

TYPE:
ROCK-STEEL

Probopass uses the strong magnetic field it generates to control the three smaller Mini-Noses attached to the sides of its body.

Nosepass   Probopass

QWILFISH

Balloon Pokémon

How to say it: KWILL-fish

Height: 1' 08"   **Weight:** 8.6 lbs.

Possible Moves: Fell Stinger, Hydro Pump, Destiny Bond, Water Gun, Spikes, Tackle, Poison Sting, Harden, Minimize, Bubble, Rollout, Toxic Spikes, Stockpile, Spit Up, Revenge, Brine, Pin Missile, Take Down, Aqua Tail, Poison Jab

Qwilfish's body bristles all over with venomous spikes. When it puffs itself up by rapidly sucking in large quantities of water, the spikes shoot outward.

TYPE:
WATER-POISON

Does not evolve

RELICANTH
Longevity Pokémon

TYPE:
WATER-
ROCK

How to say it: REL-uh-canth

Height: 3' 03"
Weight: 51.6 lbs.

Possible Moves: Head Smash, Hydro Pump, Ancient Power, Mud Sport, Tackle, Harden, Water Gun, Rock Tomb, Yawn, Take Down, Double-Edge, Dive, Rest

The ancient Pokémon Relicanth has existed for a hundred million years without changing. Deep-sea explorers discovered it at the bottom of the ocean.

Does not evolve

REMORAID
Jet Pokémon

How to say it: REM-oh-raid

Height: 2' 00"
Weight: 26.5 lbs.

TYPE:
WATER

Possible Moves: Water Gun, Lock-On, Psybeam, Aurora Beam, Bubble Beam, Focus Energy, Water Pulse, Signal Beam, Ice Beam, Bullet Seed, Hydro Pump, Hyper Beam, Soak

Remoraid is a master marksman, using sprays of water to shoot down moving targets hundreds of feet away. It often attaches itself to a Mantine in hopes of sharing a meal.

Remoraid   Octillery

REUNICLUS

Multiplying Pokémon

How to say it: ree-yoo-NIH-klus

Height: 3' 03"   **Weight:** 44.3 lbs.

Possible Moves: Psywave, Reflect, Rollout, Snatch, Hidden Power, Light Screen, Charm, Recover, Psyshock, Endeavor, Future Sight, Pain Split, Psychic, Dizzy Punch, Skill Swap, Heal Block, Wonder Room

Reuniclus shake hands with each other to create a network between their brains. Working together boosts their psychic power, and they can crush huge rocks with their minds.

TYPE:
PSYCHIC

Solosis   Duosion   Reuniclus

RHYDON

Drill Pokémon

TYPE:
GROUND-
ROCK

How to say it: RYE-don

Height: 6' 03"   **Weight:** 264.6 lbs.

Possible Moves: Megahorn, Horn Drill, Horn Attack, Tail Whip, Stomp, Fury Attack, Scary Face, Rock Blast, Bulldoze, Chip Away, Take Down, Hammer Arm, Drill Run, Stone Edge, Earthquake

After evolving, Rhydon begins to walk upright. Its horn is strong enough to drill through boulders, and its hide is thick enough to protect it from molten lava.

Rhyhorn   Rhydon   Rhyperior

RHYHORN

Spikes Pokémon

TYPE:
GROUND-
ROCK

How to say it: RYE-horn

Height: 3' 03"
Weight: 253.5 lbs.

Possible Moves: Horn Attack, Tail Whip, Stomp, Fury Attack, Scary Face, Rock Blast, Bulldoze, Chip Away, Take Down, Drill Run, Stone Edge, Earthquake, Horn Drill, Megahorn

When Rhyhorn charges, look out! It's strong enough to knock down a building, and because of its short legs, it has trouble changing direction.

Rhyhorn　　Rhydon　　Rhyperior

RHYPERIOR

Drill Pokémon

TYPE:
GROUND-
ROCK

How to say it: rye-PEER-ee-or

Height: 7' 10"
Weight: 623.5 lbs.

Possible Moves: Rock Wrecker, Megahorn, Horn Drill, Poison Jab, Horn Attack, Tail Whip, Stomp, Fury Attack, Scary Face, Rock Blast, Chip Away, Take Down, Hammer Arm, Drill Run, Stone Edge, Earthquake

Rhyperior uses the holes in its hands to bombard its opponents with rocks. Sometimes it even hurls a Geodude! Rhyperior's rocky hide is thick enough to protect it from molten lava.

Rhyhorn　　Rhydon　　Rhyperior

ROGGENROLA

Mantle Pokémon

TYPE:
ROCK

How to say it: rah-gen-ROH-lah

Height: 1' 04"   **Weight:** 39.7 lbs.

Possible Moves: Tackle, Harden, Sand Attack, Headbutt, Rock Blast, Mud-Slap, Iron Defense, Smack Down, Rock Slide, Stealth Rock, Sandstorm, Stone Edge, Explosion

Each Roggenrola has an energy core at its center. The intense pressure in their underground home has compressed their bodies into a steely toughness.

Roggenrola   Boldore   Gigalith

SABLEYE

Darkness Pokémon

How to say it: SAY-bull-eye

Height: 1' 08"
Weight: 24.3 lbs.

Possible Moves: Mean Look, Zen Headbutt, Leer, Scratch, Foresight, Night Shade, Astonish, Fury Swipes, Fake Out, Detect, Shadow Sneak, Knock Off, Feint Attack, Punishment, Shadow Claw, Power Gem, Confuse Ray, Foul Play, Shadow Ball

Sableye lives in dark caves, where it digs up tasty gems to eat. Its gemstone eyes are influenced by its diet.

Does not evolve

SALAMENCE

Dragon Pokémon

How to say it: SAL-uh-mence

Height: 4' 11"
Weight: 226.2 lbs.

TYPE:
DRAGON-FIGHTING

Possible Moves: Double-Edge, Fire Fang, Thunder Fang, Rage, Bite, Leer, Headbutt, Focus Energy, Ember, Protect, Dragon Breath, Zen Headbutt, Scary Face, Fly, Crunch, Dragon Claw, Dragon Tail

Salamence poses a serious threat to everything around it if it becomes enraged. Its fits of fiery destruction cannot be controlled.

Bagon   Shelgon   Salamence

SANDILE

Desert Croc Pokémon

How to say it: SAN-dyle

Height: 2' 04"
Weight: 33.5 lbs.

Possible Moves: Leer, Rage, Bite, Sand Attack, Torment, Sand Tomb, Assurance, Mud-Slap, Embargo, Swagger, Crunch, Dig, Scary Face, Foul Play, Sandstorm, Earthquake, Thrash

Sandile travels just below the surface of the desert sand, with only its nose and eyes sticking out. The warmth of the sand keeps it from getting too cold.

Sandile   Krokorok   Krookodile

SAWK

Karate Pokémon

TYPE:
FIGHTING

How to say it: SAWK

Height: 4' 07"   **Weight:** 112.4 lbs.

Possible Moves: Rock Smash, Leer, Bide, Focus Energy, Double Kick, Low Sweep, Counter, Karate Chop, Brick Break, Bulk Up, Retaliate, Endure, Quick Guard, Close Combat, Reversal

Sawk go deep into the mountains to train their fighting skills relentlessly. If they are disturbed during this training, they become very angry.

Does not evolve

SEADRA
Dragon Pokémon

How to say it: SEE-dra

Height: 3' 11"   **Weight:** 55.1 lbs.

Possible Moves: Water Gun, Smokescreen, Leer, Bubble, Focus Energy, Bubble Beam, Agility, Twister, Brine, Hydro Pump, Dragon Dance, Dragon Pulse

The bristling spikes that cover Seadra's body are very sharp, so touching it is not recommended. It can swim in reverse by flapping its large fins.

TYPE:
WATER

Horsea   Seadra   Kingdra

SEVIPER
Fang Snake Pokémon

TYPE:
POISON

How to say it: seh-VIE-per

Height: 8' 10"   **Weight:** 115.7 lbs.

Possible Moves: Wrap, Swagger, Bite, Lick, Poison Tail, Screech, Venoshock, Glare, Poison Fang, Venom Drench, Night Slash, Gastro Acid, Haze, Poison Jab, Crunch, Belch, Coil, Wring Out

Seviper keeps the blade on its poisonous tail polished to a razor-sharp edge. These Pokémon constantly feud with Zangoose.

Does not evolve

SHELGON
Endurance Pokémon

TYPE: DRAGON

How to say it: SHELL-gon

Height: 3' 07"　**Weight:** 243.6 lbs.

Possible Moves: Rage, Bite, Leer, Headbutt, Focus Energy, Ember, Protect, Dragon Breath, Zen Headbutt, Scary Face, Crunch, Dragon Claw, Double-Edge

The heavy, armored shell that encases Shelgon's body protects it from attacks, but also makes it move slowly.

Bagon　Shelgon　Salamence

SHELLDER
Bivalve Pokémon

TYPE: WATER

How to say it: SHELL-der

Height: 1' 00"　**Weight:** 8.8 lbs.

Possible Moves: Tackle, Withdraw, Supersonic, Icicle Spear, Protect, Leer, Clamp, Ice Shard, Razor Shell, Aurora Beam, Whirlpool, Brine, Iron Defense, Ice Beam, Shell Smash, Hydro Pump

When Shellder's shell is open, its soft body is vulnerable to attacks. After opening, it can clamp down fiercely on an opponent, but the risk is often too great.

Shellder　Cloyster

SIGILYPH

Avianoid Pokémon

TYPE:
PSYCHIC-
FLYING

How to say it: SIH-jih-liff

Height: 4' 07"
Weight: 30.9 lbs.

Possible Moves: Gust, Miracle Eye, Hypnosis, Psywave, Tailwind, Whirlwind, Psybeam, Air Cutter, Light Screen, Reflect, Synchronoise, Mirror Move, Gravity, Air Slash, Psychic, Cosmic Power, Sky Attack

Sigilyph were appointed to keep watch over an ancient city. Their patrol route never varies.

Does not evolve

SKRELP

Mock Kelp Pokémon

How to say it: SKRELP

Height: 1' 08"   **Weight:** 16.1 lbs.

Possible Moves: Tackle, Smokescreen, Water Gun, Feint Attack, Tail Whip, Bubble, Acid, Camouflage, Poison Tail, Water Pulse, Double Team, Toxic, Aqua Tail, Sludge Bomb, Hydro Pump, Dragon Pulse

Skrelp disguises itself as rotten kelp to hide from enemies. It defends itself by spraying a poisonous liquid.

TYPE:
POISON-
WATER

Skrelp   Dragalge

SKUNTANK
Skunk Pokémon

How to say it: SKUN-tank

Height: 3' 03"
Weight: 83.8 lbs.

Possible Moves: Scratch, Focus Energy, Poison Gas, Screech, Fury Swipes, Smokescreen, Feint, Slash, Toxic, Acid Spray, Flamethrower, Night Slash, Memento, Belch, Explosion

From the end of its tail, Skuntank can shoot a noxious fluid more than 160 feet. This fluid smells awful, and the stench only gets worse if it's not cleaned up immediately.

TYPE:
POISON-DARK

Stunky ➡ **Skuntank**

SLOWBRO
Hermit Crab Pokémon

How to say it: SLOW-bro

TYPE:
WATER-PSYCHIC

Height: 5' 03"
Weight: 173.1 lbs.

Possible Moves: Heal Pulse, Curse, Yawn, Tackle, Growl, Water Gun, Confusion, Disable, Headbutt, Water Pulse, Zen Headbutt, Slack Off, Withdraw, Amnesia, Psychic, Rain Dance, Psych Up

Apparently, Slowbro's tail is very tasty, so the biting Shellder will never let go.

Slowpoke ➡ **Slowbro**

SLOWKING
Royal Pokémon

TYPE:
WATER-PSYCHIC

How to say it: SLOW-king

Height: 6' 07"   **Weight:** 175.3 lbs.

Possible Moves: Heal Pulse, Power Gem, Hidden Power, Curse, Yawn, Tackle, Growl, Water Gun, Confusion, Disable, Headbutt, Water Pulse, Zen Headbutt, Nasty Plot, Swagger, Psychic, Trump Card, Psych Up

Being bitten in the head had the unusual effect of focusing Slowking's mind. Its intelligence and intuition are impressive.

Slowpoke   Slowking

SLOWPOKE
Dopey Pokémon

TYPE:
WATER-PSYCHIC

How to say it: SLOW-poke

Height: 3' 11"   **Weight:** 79.4 lbs.

Possible Moves: Curse, Yawn, Tackle, Growl, Water Gun, Confusion, Disable, Headbutt, Water Pulse, Zen Headbutt, Slack Off, Amnesia, Psychic, Rain Dance, Psych Up, Heal Pulse

Slowpoke uses its tail for fishing, but it's often too distracted to notice when it gets a bite. No one knows what it daydreams about all day long.

Slowbro

Slowpoke   Slowking

SNUBBULL

Fairy Pokémon

TYPE:
FAIRY

How to say it: SNUB-bull

Height: 2' 00"
Weight: 17.2 lbs.

Possible Moves: Ice Fang, Fire Fang, Thunder Fang, Tackle, Scary Face, Tail Whip, Charm, Bite, Lick, Headbutt, Roar, Rage, Play Rough, Payback, Crunch

Snubbull's scary face hides an affectionate and playful side. Many people think it's cute despite its fierce expression.

Snubbull Granbull

SOLOSIS

Cell Pokémon

TYPE:
PSYCHIC

How to say it: soh-LOH-sis

Height: 1' 00"   **Weight:** 2.2 lbs.

Possible Moves: Psywave, Reflect, Rollout, Snatch, Hidden Power, Light Screen, Charm, Recover, Psyshock, Endeavor, Future Sight, Pain Split, Psychic, Skill Swap, Heal Block, Wonder Room

The special liquid that surrounds Solosis protects it from any harsh conditions. They communicate with telepathy.

Solosis   Duosion   Reuniclus

SOLROCK
Meteorite Pokémon

How to say it: SOLE-rock

Height: 3' 11"
Weight: 339.5 lbs.

Possible Moves: Wonder Room, Rock Throw, Tackle, Harden, Confusion, Fire Spin, Rock Polish, Psywave, Embargo, Rock Slide, Cosmic Power, Psychic, Heal Block, Stone Edge, Solar Beam, Explosion

Solrock soaks up the sun's rays during the day to keep itself powered up. Its body gives off a sunny glow when it spins.

TYPE:
ROCK-PSYCHIC

Does not evolve

SPOINK
Bounce Pokémon

How to say it: SPOINK

Height: 2' 04"   **Weight:** 67.5 lbs.

Possible Moves: Splash, Psywave, Odor Sleuth, Psybeam, Psych Up, Confuse Ray, Magic Coat, Zen Headbutt, Rest, Snore, Power Gem, Psyshock, Payback, Psychic, Bounce

The constant bouncing motion of Spoink's springy tail regulates its heartbeat. The pearl on its forehead was produced by a Clamperl.

TYPE:
PSYCHIC

Spoink   Grumpig

STARAPTOR

Predator Pokémon

How to say it: star-RAP-tor

Height: 3' 11"
Weight: 54.9 lbs.

Possible Moves: Tackle, Growl, Quick Attack, Wing Attack, Double Team, Endeavor, Whirlwind, Aerial Ace, Take Down, Close Combat, Agility, Brave Bird, Final Gambit

After evolving, Staraptor go off on their own, leaving their flocks behind. With their strong wings, they can fly with ease even when carrying a burden.

TYPE:
NORMAL-FLYING

Starly   Staravia   Staraptor

STARAVIA

Starling Pokémon

TYPE:
NORMAL-FLYING

How to say it: star-AY-vee-ah

Height: 2' 00"
Weight: 34.2 lbs.

Possible Moves: Tackle, Growl, Quick Attack, Wing Attack, Double Team, Endeavor, Whirlwind, Aerial Ace, Take Down, Agility, Brave Bird, Final Gambit

Staravia travel in large flocks that can be very territorial. Battles sometimes break out between two competing flocks.

Starly   Staravia   Staraptor

STARLY
Starling Pokémon

TYPE:
NORMAL-
FLYING

How to say it: STAR-lee

Height: 1' 00"   **Weight:** 4.4 lbs.

Possible Moves: Tackle, Growl, Quick Attack, Wing Attack, Double Team, Endeavor, Whirlwind, Aerial Ace, Take Down, Agility, Brave Bird, Final Gambit

Huge flocks of Starly gather in fields and mountains. In such large numbers, their wings flap with impressive power . . . and their noisy singing is quite a nuisance!

Starly   Staravia   Staraptor

STARMIE
Mysterious Pokémon

How to say it: STAR-mee

Height: 3' 07"
Weight: 176.4 lbs.

TYPE:
WATER-
PSYCHIC

Possible Moves: Hydro Pump, Water Gun, Rapid Spin, Recover, Swift, Confuse Ray

The gemlike core at Starmie's center emits light of many colors. It is also thought to produce radio waves at night.

Staryu   Starmie

STARYU
Star Shape Pokémon

How to say it: STAR-you

Height: 2' 07"　**Weight:** 76.1 lbs.

TYPE: WATER

Possible Moves: Tackle, Harden, Water Gun, Rapid Spin, Recover, Camouflage, Swift, Bubble Beam, Minimize, Gyro Ball, Light Screen, Brine, Reflect Type, Power Gem, Cosmic Power, Hydro Pump

The red core at the middle of Staryu's body can be seen flashing at night. As long as this core is whole, it can regenerate from any damage.

Staryu　　Starmie

STEELIX
Iron Snake Pokémon

How to say it: STEE-licks

Height: 30' 02"
Weight: 881.8 lbs.

Possible Moves:
Thunder Fang, Ice Fang, Fire Fang, Mud Sport, Tackle, Harden, Bind, Curse, Rock Throw, Rock Tomb, Rage, Stealth Rock, Autotomize, Gyro Ball, Smack Down, Dragon Breath, Slam, Screech, Rock Slide, Crunch, Iron Tail, Dig, Stone Edge, Double-Edge, Sandstorm

TYPE: STEEL-GROUND

Steelix lives deep underground, where intense heat and pressure have compressed its body to a steely toughness. It can crunch large rocks in its jaws.

Onix　　　Steelix

STUNKY
Skunk Pokémon

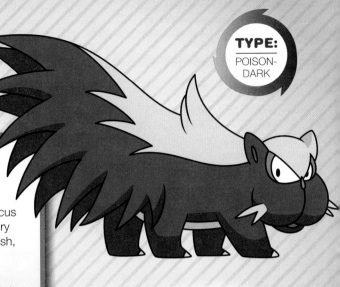

TYPE:
POISON-
DARK

How to say it: STUNK-ee

Height: 1' 04"
Weight: 42.3 lbs.

Possible Moves: Scratch, Focus Energy, Poison Gas, Screech, Fury Swipes, Smokescreen, Feint, Slash, Toxic, Acid Spray, Night Slash, Memento, Belch, Explosion

The terrible-smelling fluid that Stunky sprays from its rear can keep others far away from it for a whole day.

Stunky   Skuntank

SWELLOW
Swallow Pokémon

How to say it: SWELL-low

Height: 2' 04"   **Weight:** 43.7 lbs.

Possible Moves: Air Slash, Pluck, Peck, Growl, Focus Energy, Quick Attack, Wing Attack, Double Team, Endeavor, Aerial Ace, Agility

Soaring gracefully through the sky, Swellow will go into a steep dive if it spots food on the ground. Its prominent tail feathers stand straight up when it's in good health.

TYPE:
NORMAL-
FLYING

Taillow   Swellow

SWOOBAT
Courting Pokémon

How to say it: SWOO-bat

Height: 2' 11" **Weight:** 23.1 lbs.

Possible Moves: Confusion, Odor Sleuth, Gust, Assurance, Heart Stamp, Imprison, Air Cutter, Attract, Amnesia, Calm Mind, Air Slash, Future Sight, Psychic, Endeavor

When a male Swoobat is trying to impress a female, it gives off ultrasonic waves that put everyone in a good mood. Under other circumstances, Swoobat's waves can pulverize concrete.

TYPE:
PSYCHIC-FLYING

Woobat → Swoobat

SYLVEON
Intertwining Pokémon

TYPE:
FAIRY

How to say it: SIL-vee-on

Height: 3' 03" **Weight:** 51.8 lbs.

Possible Moves: Disarming Voice, Tail Whip, Tackle, Helping Hand, Sand Attack, Fairy Wind, Quick Attack, Swift, Draining Kiss, Skill Swap, Misty Terrain, Light Screen, Moonblast, Last Resort, Psych Up

To keep others from fighting, Sylveon projects a calming aura from its feelers, which look like flowing ribbons. It wraps those ribbons around its Trainer's arm when they walk together.

Eevee → Sylveon

TAILLOW
Tiny Swallow Pokémon

How to say it: TAY-low

Height: 1' 00"
Weight: 5.1 lbs.

Possible Moves: Peck, Growl, Focus Energy, Quick Attack, Wing Attack, Double Team, Endeavor, Aerial Ace, Agility, Air Slash

Taillow don't like the cold and will fly nearly two hundred miles in a single day to seek out a warmer home. They show real fighting spirit in battle, even against tough opponents.

TYPE: NORMAL-FLYING

Taillow   Swellow

TAUROS
Wild Bull Pokémon

TYPE: NORMAL

How to say it: TORE-ros

Height: 4' 07"
Weight: 194.9 lbs.

Possible Moves: Tackle, Tail Whip, Rage, Horn Attack, Scary Face, Pursuit, Rest, Payback, Work Up, Zen Headbutt, Take Down, Swagger, Thrash, Giga Impact

To get pumped up for a fight, Tauros whips itself with its three tails. This is a sure sign that it's about to charge.

Does not evolve

TENTACOOL
Jellyfish Pokémon

How to say it: TEN-ta-cool

Height: 2' 11"   **Weight:** 100.3 lbs.

Possible Moves: Poison Sting, Supersonic, Constrict, Acid, Toxic Spikes, Bubble Beam, Wrap, Acid Spray, Barrier, Water Pulse, Poison Jab, Screech, Hex, Hydro Pump, Sludge Wave, Wring Out

Water makes up most of Tentacool's body. It drifts with the current in areas where the sea is shallow.

TYPE:
WATER-
POISON

Tentacool → Tentacruel

TENTACRUEL
Jellyfish Pokémon

How to say it: TEN-ta-crool

Height: 5' 03"   **Weight:** 121.3 lbs.

Possible Moves: Reflect Type, Wring Out, Poison Sting, Supersonic, Constrict, Acid, Toxic Spikes, Bubble Beam, Wrap, Acid Spray, Barrier, Water Pulse, Poison Jab, Screech, Hex, Hydro Pump, Sludge Wave

Eighty tentacles equipped with painful venom extend from Tentacruel's body. It can pull them in to make itself smaller, or lengthen them to attack.

TYPE:
WATER-
POISON

Tentacool → Tentacruel

THROH
Judo Pokémon

TYPE:
FIGHTING

How to say it: THROH

Height: 4' 03"   **Weight:** 122.4 lbs.

Possible Moves: Bind, Leer, Bide, Focus Energy, Seismic Toss, Vital Throw, Revenge, Storm Throw, Body Slam, Bulk Up, Circle Throw, Endure, Wide Guard, Superpower, Reversal

Throh make belts for themselves out of vines, and pull those belts tight to power up their muscles. They can't resist the challenge of throwing a bigger opponent.

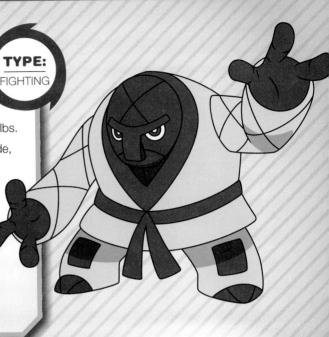

Does not evolve

TYRANTRUM
Despot Pokémon

How to say it: tie-RAN-trum

Height: 8' 02"   **Weight:** 595.2 lbs.

Possible Moves: Head Smash, Tail Whip, Tackle, Roar, Stomp, Bide, Stealth Rock, Bite, Charm, Ancient Power, Dragon Tail, Crunch, Dragon Claw, Thrash, Earthquake, Horn Drill, Head Smash, Rock Slide, Giga Impact

Tyrantrum's enormous and powerful jaws made it the boss of its ancient world. Nothing could challenge its rule.

TYPE:
ROCK-
DRAGON

Tyrunt   **Tyrantrum**

TYRUNT

Royal Heir Pokémon

How to say it: TIE-runt

Height: 2' 07"
Weight: 57.3 lbs.

Possible Moves: Tail Whip, Tackle, Roar, Stomp, Bide, Stealth Rock, Bite, Charm, Ancient Power, Dragon Tail, Crunch, Dragon Claw, Thrash, Earthquake, Horn Drill

Tyrunt often responds to frustration by pitching a fit. This ancient Pokémon lived millions of years ago.

TYPE:
ROCK-DRAGON

Tyrunt ➡ Tyrantrum

UMBREON

Moonlight Pokémon

How to say it: UM-bree-on

Height: 3' 03"
Weight: 59.5 lbs.

Possible Moves: Helping Hand, Tackle, Tail Whip, Sand Attack, Pursuit, Quick Attack, Confuse Ray, Feint Attack, Assurance, Screech, Moonlight, Mean Look, Last Resort, Guard Swap

Umbreon's genetic structure is influenced by moonlight. When the moon shines upon it, the rings in its fur give off a faint glow.

TYPE:
DARK

Eevee ➡ Umbreon

VAPOREON

Bubble Jet Pokémon

TYPE:
WATER

How to say it: vay-POUR-ree-on

Height: 3' 03"　**Weight:** 63.9 lbs.

Possible Moves: Helping Hand, Tackle, Tail Whip, Sand Attack, Water Gun, Quick Attack, Water Pulse, Aurora Beam, Aqua Ring, Acid Armor, Haze, Muddy Water, Last Resort, Hydro Pump

Vaporeon's cellular structure resembles water molecules, so it can melt away and vanish in its aquatic environment. It loves beautiful beaches.

Eevee　　Vaporeon

WAILMER

Ball Whale Pokémon

How to say it: WAIL-murr

Height: 6' 07"   **Weight:** 286.6 lbs.

Possible Moves: Splash, Growl, Water Gun, Rollout, Whirlpool, Astonish, Water Pulse, Mist, Rest, Brine, Water Spout, Amnesia, Dive, Bounce, Hydro Pump, Heavy Slam

Wailmer swallows seawater to make its round body even rounder and its playful bounces even higher. It releases the seawater in a forceful spray from its blowholes.

Wailmer   Wailord

WAILORD

Float Whale Pokémon

TYPE:
WATER

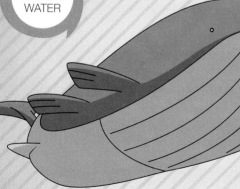

How to say it: WAI-lord

Height: 47' 07"
Weight: 877.4 lbs.

Possible Moves: Splash, Growl, Water Gun, Rollout, Whirlpool, Astonish, Water Pulse, Mist, Rest, Brine, Water Spout, Amnesia, Dive, Bounce, Hydro Pump, Heavy Slam

When Wailord leaps from the water in a mighty breach and then crashes down again, the shock wave it creates is sometimes enough to knock an opponent out.

Wailmer   Wailord

WINGULL

Seagull Pokémon

TYPE:
WATER-
FLYING

How to say it: WING-gull

Height: 2' 00"
Weight: 20.9 lbs.

Possible Moves: Growl, Water Gun, Supersonic, Wing Attack, Mist, Water Pulse, Quick Attack, Roost, Pursuit, Air Cutter, Agility, Aerial Ace, Air Slash, Hurricane

Wingull build nests on the sides of steep cliffs by the sea. Stretching out their long wings, they soar on the ocean breeze.

Wingull → Pelipper

WOBBUFFET

Patient Pokémon

TYPE:
PSYCHIC

How to say it: WAH-buf-fett

Height: 4' 03"   **Weight:** 62.8 lbs.

Possible Moves: Counter, Mirror Coat, Safeguard, Destiny Bond

Wobbuffet prefers to hide in dark places, where its black tail can't be seen, and avoids battle when possible. If another Pokémon attacks it first, it puffs up its body and strikes back.

Wynaut → Wobbuffet

How to say it: WOO-bat

Height: 1' 04"
Weight: 4.6 lbs.

Possible Moves:
Confusion, Odor Sleuth, Gust, Assurance, Heart Stamp, Imprison, Air Cutter, Attract, Amnesia, Calm Mind, Air Slash, Future Sight, Psychic, Endeavor

When Woobat attaches itself to something, it leaves a heart-shaped mark with its nose. The nose is also the source of its echolocation signals.

TYPE:
PSYCHIC-FLYING

Woobat   Swoobat

How to say it: WHY-not

Height: 2' 00"
Weight: 30.9 lbs.

Possible Moves: Splash, Charm, Encore, Counter, Mirror Coat, Safeguard, Destiny Bond

When it's time to sleep, a group of Wynaut find a cave and snuggle up close together. Sweet berries are their favorite food.

TYPE:
PSYCHIC

Wynaut   Wobbuffet

YANMA
Clear Wing Pokémon

TYPE:
BUG-FLYING

How to say it: YAN-ma

Height: 3' 11"   **Weight:** 83.8 lbs.

Possible Moves: Tackle, Foresight, Quick Attack, Double Team, Sonic Boom, Detect, Supersonic, Uproar, Pursuit, Ancient Power, Hypnosis, Wing Attack, Screech, U-turn, Air Slash, Bug Buzz

With its compound eyes, Yanma can see in every direction without moving its head. It can send out a shock wave from its rapidly buzzing wings.

Yanma   Yanmega

YANMEGA
Ogre Darner Pokémon

How to say it: yan-MEG-ah

Height: 6' 03"   **Weight:** 113.5 lbs.

Possible Moves: Bug Buzz, Air Slash, Night Slash, Bug Bite, Tackle, Foresight, Quick Attack, Double Team, Sonic Boom, Detect, Supersonic, Uproar, Pursuit, Ancient Power, Feint, Slash, Screech, U-turn

With four wings on its back and two more on its tail to keep it balanced, Yanmega is capable of extremely high-speed flight. It can carry a full-grown person through the air.

TYPE:
BUG-FLYING

Yanma   Yanmega

ZANGOOSE
Cat Ferret Pokémon

How to say it: ZANG-goose

Height: 4' 03"
Weight: 88.8 lbs.

Possible Moves:
Scratch, Leer, Quick Attack, Fury Cutter, Pursuit, Slash, Embargo, Crush Claw, Revenge, False Swipe, Detect, X-Scissor, Taunt, Swords Dance, Close Combat

When Zangoose smells an enemy, its fur bristles up and it wields its sharp claws. These Pokémon constantly feud with Seviper.

Does not evolve

TYPE:
NORMAL

LEGENDARY POKÉMON

ZAPDOS
Electric Pokémon

How to say it: ZAP-dose

Height: 5' 03"
Weight: 116.0 lbs.

Possible Moves: Roost, Zap Cannon, Drill Peck, Peck, Thunder Shock, Thunder Wave, Detect, Pluck, Ancient Power, Charge, Agility, Discharge, Rain Dance, Light Screen, Thunder

It is said that Zapdos lives in thunderclouds. This Legendary Pokémon can control lightning and fling bolts at the ground.

TYPE:
ELECTRIC-FLYING

Does not evolve

Welcome to the Kalos Mountain Subregion!

Greetings from the highest points in all of Kalos! This subregion is filled with icy natural beauty. It's known for Victory Road and the world-famous Poké Ball Factory.

The biggest attractions in the mountain subregion are the Pokémon. Here you'll find Dragon-type Pokémon such as Garchomp, Noivern, and Goomy, plus Ghost-type and Poison-type Pokémon like Gengar, Litwick, and Trevenant. And of course, the mountain peaks are packed with Ice-type Pokémon, including Vanilluxe, Mamoswine, and Bergmite.

ABOMASNOW
Frost Tree Pokémon

How to say it: ah-BOM-ah-snow

Height: 7' 03"
Weight: 298.7 lbs.

Possible Moves: Ice Punch, Powder Snow, Leer, Razor Leaf, Icy Wind, Grass Whistle, Swagger, Mist, Ice Shard, Ingrain, Wood Hammer, Blizzard, Sheer Cold

Snow-covered mountains are Abomasnow's preferred habitat. It creates blizzards to hide itself and keep others away.

TYPE:
GRASS-ICE

MEGA ABOMASNOW
Frost Tree Pokémon

Height: 8' 10"
Weight: 407.9 lbs.

TYPE:
GRASS-ICE

Snover → Abomasnow → Mega Abomasnow

ACCELGOR

Shell Out Pokémon

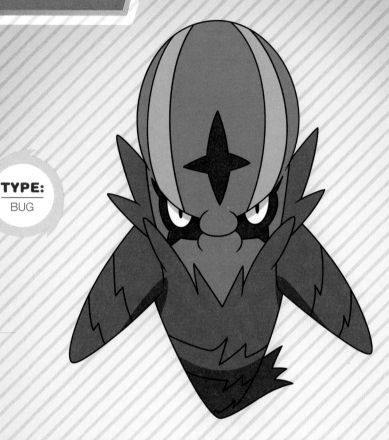

TYPE:

BUG

How to say it: ak-SELL-gohr

Height: 2' 07"   **Weight:** 55.8 lbs.

Possible Moves: Final Gambit, Power Swap, Leech Life, Acid Spray, Double Team, Quick Attack, Struggle Bug, Mega Drain, Swift, Me First, Agility, Giga Drain, U-turn, Bug Buzz, Recover

After coming out of its shell, Accelgor is light and quick, moving with the speed of a ninja. It wraps its body up to keep from drying out.

Shelmet   Accelgor

AGGRON

Iron Armor Pokémon

TYPE:
STEEL-ROCK

How to say it: AGG-ron

Height: 6' 11"
Weight: 793.7 lbs.

Possible Moves: Tackle, Harden, Mud-Slap, Headbutt, Metal Claw, Iron Defense, Roar, Take Down, Iron Head, Protect, Metal Sound, Iron Tail, Autotomize, Heavy Slam, Double-Edge, Metal Burst

With horns of steel, Aggron can dig tunnels through solid rock in search of iron ore to eat.

MEGA AGGRON

Iron Armor Pokémon

Height: 7' 03"
Weight: 870.8 lbs.

TYPE:
STEEL-ROCK

Aron → Lairon → Aggron → Mega Aggron

ALTARIA
Humming Pokémon

TYPE:
DRAGON-
FLYING

How to say it: ahl-TAR-ee-uh

Height: 3' 07"   **Weight:** 45.4 lbs.

Possible Moves: Sky Attack, Pluck, Peck, Growl, Astonish, Sing, Fury Attack, Safeguard, Mist, Round, Natural Gift, Take Down, Refresh, Dragon Dance, Dragon Breath, Cotton Guard, Dragon Pulse, Perish Song, Moonblast

In its lovely soprano voice, Altaria sings sweetly as it flies through sunny skies. It is often mistaken for a passing cloud.

Swablu   Altaria

AMOONGUSS
Mushroom Pokémon

TYPE:
GRASS-
POISON

How to say it: uh-MOON-gus

Height: 2' 00"   **Weight:** 23.1 lbs.

Possible Moves: Absorb, Growth, Astonish, Bide, Mega Drain, Ingrain, Feint Attack, Sweet Scent, Giga Drain, Toxic, Synthesis, Clear Smog, Solar Beam, Rage Powder, Spore

In a swaying dance, Amoonguss waves its arm caps, which look like Poké Balls, in an attempt to lure the unwary. It doesn't often work.

Foongus   Amoonguss

ARBOK
Cobra Pokémon

How to say it: ARE-bock

Height: 11' 06" **Weight:** 143.3 lbs.

Possible Moves: Ice Fang, Thunder Fang, Fire Fang, Wrap, Leer, Poison Sting, Bite, Glare, Screech, Acid, Crunch, Stockpile, Swallow, Spit Up, Acid Spray, Mud Bomb, Gastro Acid, Belch, Haze, Coil, Gunk Shot

When threatened, Arbok flares its hood to expose its belly pattern, which looks like a scary face. This is often enough to make enemies run away.

TYPE:
POISON

Ekans → Arbok

ARIADOS
Long Leg Pokémon

How to say it: AIR-ree-uh-dose

Height: 3' 07"
Weight: 73.9 lbs.

Possible Moves: Venom Drench, Fell Stinger, Bug Bite, Poison Sting, String Shot, Scary Face, Constrict, Leech Life, Night Shade, Shadow Sneak, Fury Swipes, Sucker Punch, Spider Web, Agility, Pin Missile, Psychic, Poison Jab, Cross Poison, Sticky Web

Ariados spins thread for its web from both ends of its body. It sometimes tracks its prey by means of this thread.

TYPE:
BUG-POISON

Spinarak → Ariados

ARON
Iron Armor Pokémon

TYPE:
STEEL-ROCK

How to say it: AIR-ron

Height: 1' 04"   **Weight:** 132.3 lbs.

Possible Moves: Tackle, Harden, Mud-Slap, Headbutt, Metal Claw, Iron Defense, Roar, Take Down, Iron Head, Protect, Metal Sound, Iron Tail, Autotomize, Heavy Slam, Double-Edge, Metal Burst

When Aron can't find enough food in its mountain home, it might resort to chewing up railroad tracks.

Aron   Lairon   Aggron   Mega Aggron

AVALUGG
Iceberg Pokémon

TYPE:
ICE

How to say it: AV-uh-lug

Height: 6' 07"   **Weight:** 1,113.3 lbs.

Possible Moves: Iron Defense, Crunch, Skull Bash, Tackle, Bite, Harden, Powder Snow, Icy Wind, Take Down, Sharpen, Curse, Ice Fang, Ice Ball, Rapid Spin, Avalanche, Blizzard, Recover, Double-Edge

Avalugg's broad, flat back is a common resting place for groups of Bergmite. Its big, bulky body can crush obstacles in its path.

Bergmite   Avalugg

BANETTE

Marionette Pokémon

How to say it: bane-NETT

Height: 3' 07"
Weight: 27.6 lbs.

Possible Moves: Knock Off, Screech, Night Shade, Curse, Spite, Will-O-Wisp, Shadow Sneak, Feint Attack, Hex, Shadow Ball, Sucker Punch, Embargo, Snatch, Grudge, Trick

Banette used to be a child's plaything. When it was thrown out, it became a Pokémon out of spite toward its former owner.

TYPE:
GHOST

MEGA BANETTE

Marionette Pokémon

Height: 3' 11"
Weight: 28.7 lbs.

TYPE:
GHOST

Shuppet → **Banette** → **Mega Banette**

BARBOACH
Whiskers Pokémon

TYPE:
WATER-
GROUND

How to say it: bar-BOACH

Height: 1' 04"
Weight: 4.2 lbs.

Possible Moves: Mud-Slap, Mud Sport, Water Sport, Water Gun, Mud Bomb, Amnesia, Water Pulse, Magnitude, Rest, Snore, Aqua Tail, Earthquake, Future Sight, Fissure

Barboach is covered in a slippery slime, so it's difficult for an opponent to get a good grip. It uses its whiskers to sense its surroundings in places where the water isn't clear.

Barboach   Whiscash

BASCULIN
Hostile Pokémon

Red Stripe

How to say it: BASS-kyoo-lin

Height: 3' 03"   **Weight:** 39.7 lbs.

Possible Moves: Thrash, Flail, Tail Whip, Tackle, Water Gun, Uproar, Headbutt, Bite, Aqua Jet, Chip Away, Take Down, Crunch, Aqua Tail, Soak, Double-Edge, Scary Face, Final Gambit

An ongoing feud exists between Basculin with blue stripes and Basculin with red stripes. Because they're constantly fighting, they are rarely found in the same place.

TYPE:
WATER

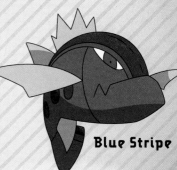

Blue Stripe

Does not evolve

BEARTIC

Freezing Pokémon

How to say it: BAIR-tick

Height: 8' 06"
Weight: 573.2 lbs.

Possible Moves: Sheer Cold, Thrash, Superpower, Aqua Jet, Growl, Powder Snow, Bide, Icy Wind, Play Nice, Fury Swipes, Brine, Endure, Swagger, Slash, Flail, Icicle Crash, Rest, Blizzard, Hail

Beartic live in the far north, where the seas are very cold. Their fangs and claws are made of ice formed by their own freezing breath.

TYPE:
ICE

Cubchoo ➡ Beartic

BELLSPROUT

Flower Pokémon

How to say it: BELL-sprout

Height: 2' 04"   **Weight:** 8.8 lbs.

Possible Moves: Vine Whip, Growth, Wrap, Sleep Powder, Poison Powder, Stun Spore, Acid, Knock Off, Sweet Scent, Gastro Acid, Razor Leaf, Slam, Wring Out

Bellsprout's flower resembles a face. Its stalklike body can move at unexpected speeds when it's chasing something.

TYPE:
GRASS-POISON

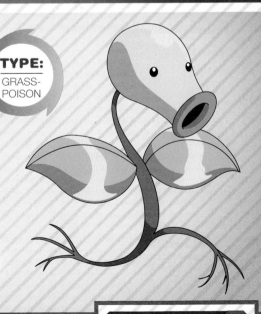

Bellsprout ➡ Weepinbell ➡ Victreebel

BERGMITE

Ice Chunk Pokémon

How to say it: BERG-mite

Height: 3' 03"   **Weight:** 219.4 lbs.

Possible Moves: Tackle, Bite, Harden, Powder Snow, Icy Wind, Take Down, Sharpen, Curse, Ice Fang, Ice Ball, Rapid Spin, Avalanche, Blizzard, Recover, Double-Edge

When cracks form in Bergmite's icy body, it uses freezing air to patch itself up with new ice. It lives high in the mountains.

Bergmite   Avalugg

BISHARP

Sword Blade Pokémon

TYPE:
DARK-
STEEL

How to say it: BIH-sharp

Height: 5' 03"   **Weight:** 154.3 lbs.

Possible Moves: Guillotine, Iron Head, Metal Burst, Scratch, Leer, Fury Cutter, Torment, Feint Attack, Scary Face, Metal Claw, Slash, Assurance, Metal Sound, Embargo, Iron Defense, Night Slash, Swords Dance

When Pawniard hunt in a pack, Bisharp leads them and gives the orders. It's often the one that deals the final blow.

Pawniard   Bisharp

BONSLY
Bonsai Pokémon

TYPE:
ROCK

How to say it: BON-slye

Height: 1' 08"   **Weight:** 33.1 lbs.

Possible Moves: Fake Tears, Copycat, Flail, Low Kick, Rock Throw, Mimic, Feint Attack, Rock Tomb, Block, Rock Slide, Counter, Sucker Punch, Double-Edge

Bonsly prefers to live in dry places. When its body stores excess moisture, it releases water from its eyes, making it look like it's crying.

Bonsly   Sudowoodo

BUIZEL
Sea Weasel Pokémon

TYPE:
WATER

How to say it: BWEE-zul

Height: 2' 04"   **Weight:** 65.0 lbs.

Possible Moves: Sonic Boom, Growl, Water Sport, Quick Attack, Water Gun, Pursuit, Swift, Aqua Jet, Double Hit, Whirlpool, Razor Wind, Aqua Tail, Agility, Hydro Pump

Buizel rapidly spins its two tails to propel itself through the water. The flotation sac around its neck keeps its head up without effort, and it can deflate the sac to dive.

Buizel   Floatzel

CARNIVINE
Bug Catcher Pokémon

TYPE: GRASS

How to say it: CAR-neh-vine

Height: 4' 07"   **Weight:** 59.5 lbs.

Possible Moves: Bind, Growth, Bite, Vine Whip, Sweet Scent, Ingrain, Feint Attack, Leaf Tornado, Stockpile, Spit Up, Swallow, Crunch, Wring Out, Power Whip

Carnivine wraps itself around trees in swampy areas. It gives off a sweet aroma that lures others close, then attacks.

Does not evolve

CHANDELURE
Luring Pokémon

How to say it: shan-duh-LOOR

Height: 3' 03"
Weight: 75.6 lbs.

Possible Moves: Pain Split, Smog, Confuse Ray, Flame Burst, Hex

Chandelure's spooky flames can burn the spirit right out of someone. If that happens, the spirit becomes trapped in this world, endlessly wandering.

TYPE: GHOST-FIRE

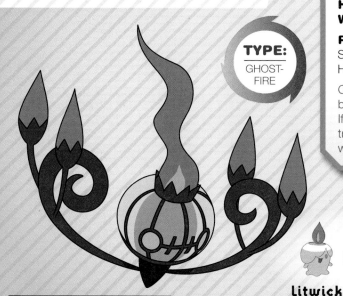

Litwick   Lampent   Chandelure

CONKELDURR
Muscular Pokémon

TYPE: FIGHTING

Timburr → Gurdurr → Conkeldurr

How to say it: kon-KELL-dur

Height: 4' 07"
Weight: 191.8 lbs.

Possible Moves: Pound, Leer, Focus Energy, Bide, Low Kick, Rock Throw, Wake-Up Slap, Chip Away, Bulk Up, Rock Slide, Dynamic Punch, Scary Face, Hammer Arm, Stone Edge, Focus Punch, Superpower

Conkeldurr spin their concrete pillars to attack. It's said that long ago, people first learned about concrete from these Pokémon.

CRYOGONAL
Crystallizing Pokémon

TYPE: ICE

How to say it: kry-AH-guh-nul

Height: 3' 07"   **Weight:** 326.3 lbs.

Possible Moves: Bind, Ice Shard, Sharpen, Rapid Spin, Icy Wind, Mist, Haze, Aurora Beam, Acid Armor, Ice Beam, Light Screen, Reflect, Slash, Confuse Ray, Recover, Solar Beam, Night Slash, Sheer Cold

Cryogonal's crystalline structure is made of ice formed in snow clouds. With its long chains of ice crystals, it unleashes a freezing attack.

Does not evolve

CUBCHOO
Chill Pokémon

TYPE:
ICE

How to say it: cub-CHOO

Height: 1' 08"
Weight: 18.7 lbs.

Possible Moves: Growl, Powder Snow, Bide, Icy Wind, Play Nice, Fury Swipes, Brine, Endure, Charm, Slash, Flail, Rest, Blizzard, Hail, Thrash, Sheer Cold

Even a healthy Cubchoo always has a runny nose. Its sniffles power its freezing attacks.

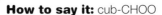

Cubchoo   Beartic

DEINO
Irate Pokémon

How to say it: DY-noh

Height: 2' 07"   **Weight:** 38.1 lbs.

Possible Moves: Tackle, Dragon Rage, Focus Energy, Bite, Headbutt, Dragon Breath, Roar, Crunch, Slam, Dragon Pulse, Work Up, Dragon Rush, Body Slam, Scary Face, Hyper Voice, Outrage

Deino can't see, so they explore their surroundings by biting and crashing into things. Because of this, they are often covered in cuts and scratches.

TYPE:
DARK-
DRAGON

Deino   Zweilous   Hydreigon

DELIBIRD

Delivery Pokémon

How to say it: DELL-ee-bird

Height: 2' 11"
Weight: 35.3 lbs.

Possible Moves: Present

Delibird stores food bundled up in its tail, so it never goes hungry when it's traveling in the mountains. It happily shares food with anyone who needs rescuing.

TYPE:
ICE-FLYING

Does not evolve

DIGLETT

Mole Pokémon

TYPE:
GROUND

How to say it: DIG-let

Height: 0' 08"
Weight: 1.8 lbs.

Possible Moves: Scratch, Sand Attack, Growl, Astonish, Mud-Slap, Magnitude, Bulldoze, Sucker Punch, Mud Bomb, Earth Power, Dig, Slash, Earthquake, Fissure

Diglett live underground to protect their thin skin from the light. They come within a few feet of the surface to munch on the roots of plants.

Diglett → Dugtrio

DITTO
Transform Pokémon

TYPE:
NORMAL

How to say it: DIT-toe

Height: 1' 00"
Weight: 8.8 lbs.

Possible Moves: Transform

Ditto rearranges the structure of its cells to alter its appearance. It can change into anything!

Does not evolve

DRAGONAIR
Dragon Pokémon

TYPE:
DRAGON

How to say it: DRAG-gon-AIR

Height: 13' 01"   **Weight:** 36.4 lbs.

Possible Moves: Wrap, Leer, Thunder Wave, Twister, Dragon Rage, Slam, Agility, Dragon Tail, Aqua Tail, Dragon Rush, Safeguard, Dragon Dance, Outrage, Hyper Beam

With the mystical orbs on its neck and tail, Dragonair is said to be able to control weather patterns.

Dratini   Dragonair   Dragonite

DRAGONITE
Dragon Pokémon

How to say it: DRAG-gon-ite

Height: 7' 03"   **Weight:** 463.0 lbs.

Possible Moves: Hurricane, Fire Punch, Thunder Punch, Roost, Wrap, Leer, Thunder Wave, Twister, Dragon Rage, Slam, Agility, Dragon Tail, Aqua Tail, Dragon Rush, Safeguard, Wing Attack, Dragon Dance, Outrage, Hyper Beam

Dragonite can fly around the whole world in less than a day. It lives far out at sea and comes to the aid of wrecked ships.

TYPE:
DRAGON

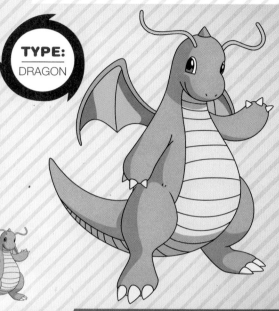

Dratini ➡ **Dragonair** ➡ **Dragonite**

DRAPION
Ogre Scorpion Pokémon

How to say it: DRAP-ee-on

Height: 4' 03"
Weight: 135.6 lbs.

Possible Moves: Thunder Fang, Ice Fang, Fire Fang, Bite, Poison Sting, Leer, Knock Off, Pin Missile, Acupressure, Pursuit, Bug Bite, Poison Fang, Venoshock, Hone Claws, Toxic Spikes, Night Slash, Scary Face, Crunch, Fell Stinger, Cross Poison

Drapion's strong arms could tear a car into scrap metal. The claws on its arms and tail are extremely toxic.

Skorupi ➡ **Drapion**

TYPE:
POISON-
DARK

DRATINI

Dragon Pokémon

TYPE:
DRAGON

How to say it: dra-TEE-nee

Height: 5' 11"   **Weight:** 7.3 lbs.

Possible Moves: Wrap, Leer, Thunder Wave, Twister, Dragon Rage, Slam, Agility, Dragon Tail, Aqua Tail, Dragon Rush, Safeguard, Dragon Dance, Outrage, Hyper Beam

Very few people have seen Dratini in the wild, so it's known as the "Mirage Pokémon." It sheds its skin several times a year as it grows.

Dratini   Dragonair   Dragoni

DRUDDIGON

Cave Pokémon

TYPE:
DRAGON

How to say it: DRUD-dih-gahn

Height: 5' 03"
Weight: 306.4 lbs.

Possible Moves: Leer, Scratch, Hone Claws, Bite, Scary Face, Dragon Rage, Slash, Crunch, Dragon Claw, Chip Away, Revenge, Night Slash, Dragon Tail, Rock Climb, Superpower, Outrage

Druddigon can't move if it gets too cold, so it soaks up the sun with its wings. It can navigate tight caves at a brisk pace.

Does not evolve

DUGTRIO
Mole Pokémon

How to say it: dug-TREE-oh

Height: 2' 04"   **Weight:** 73.4 lbs.

Possible Moves: Rototiller, Night Slash, Tri Attack, Scratch, Sand Attack, Growl, Astonish, Mud-Slap, Magnitude, Bulldoze, Sucker Punch, Sand Tomb, Mud Bomb, Earth Power, Dig, Slash, Earthquake, Fissure

During battles, Dugtrio uses its impressive burrowing skill to its advantage, striking from below, where the opponent can't see. No matter how hard the ground is, it can dig through.

TYPE:
GROUND

Diglett   Dugtrio

DURANT
Iron Ant Pokémon

TYPE:
BUG-
STEEL

How to say it: dur-ANT

Height: 1' 00"
Weight: 72.8 lbs.

Possible Moves: Guillotine, Iron Defense, Metal Sound, Vice Grip, Sand Attack, Fury Cutter, Bite, Agility, Metal Claw, Bug Bite, Crunch, Iron Head, Dig, Entrainment, X-Scissor

The heavily armored Durant work together to keep attackers away from their colony. Durant and Heatmor are natural enemies.

Does not evolve

EKANS
Snake Pokémon

TYPE: POISON

How to say it: ECK-kins

Height: 6' 07"
Weight: 15.2 lbs.

Possible Moves: Wrap, Leer, Poison Sting, Bite, Glare, Screech, Acid, Stockpile, Swallow, Spit Up, Acid Spray, Mud Bomb, Gastro Acid, Belch, Haze, Coil, Gunk Shot

You can tell how old an Ekans is by the length of its body, because it keeps growing year after year. It coils up around a branch to sleep at night.

Ekans → Arbok

ELECTRODE
Ball Pokémon

TYPE: ELECTRIC

How to say it: ee-LECK-trode

Height: 3' 11"   **Weight:** 146.8 lbs.

Possible Moves: Magnetic Flux, Charge, Tackle, Sonic Boom, Spark, Eerie Impulse, Rollout, Screech, Charge Beam, Light Screen, Electro Ball, Self-Destruct, Swift, Magnet Rise, Gyro Ball, Explosion, Mirror Coat

The electricity it stores in its body often overflows. Because of its tendency to explode at the slightest provocation, Electrode is known as "the Bomb Ball."

Voltorb   Electrode

ESCAVALIER
Cavalry Pokémon

TYPE: BUG-STEEL

How to say it: ess-KAH-vuh-LEER

Height: 3' 03"
Weight: 72.8 lbs.

Possible Moves: Double-Edge, Fell Stinger, Peck, Leer, Quick Guard, Twineedle, Fury Attack, Headbutt, False Swipe, Bug Buzz, Slash, Iron Head, Iron Defense, X-Scissor, Reversal, Swords Dance, Giga Impact

The stolen Shelmet shell protects Escavalier's body like armor. It uses its double lances to attack.

Karrablast ➡ Escavalier

FEAROW
Beak Pokémon

TYPE: NORMAL-FLYING

How to say it: FEER-oh

Height: 3' 11"
Weight: 83.8 lbs.

Possible Moves: Drill Run, Pluck, Peck, Growl, Leer, Fury Attack, Pursuit, Aerial Ace, Mirror Move, Agility, Assurance, Roost, Drill Peck

Thanks to its impressive stamina, Fearow can fly for hours without stopping for a break. Its fearsome beak is used in battle.

Spearow ➡ Fearow

FLOATZEL

Sea Weasel Pokémon

TYPE:
WATER

How to say it: FLOAT-zul

Height: 3' 07"
Weight: 73.9 lbs.

Possible Moves: Ice Fang, Crunch, Sonic Boom, Growl, Water Sport, Quick Attack, Water Gun, Pursuit, Swift, Aqua Jet, Double Hit, Whirlpool, Razor Wind, Aqua Tail, Agility, Hydro Pump

The flotation sac that surrounds its entire body makes Floatzel very good at rescuing people in the water. It can float them to safety like an inflatable raft.

Buizel ➡ Floatzel

FLYGON

Mystic Pokémon

TYPE:
GROUND-
DRAGON

How to say it: FLY-gon

Height: 6' 07"   **Weight:** 180.8 lbs.

Possible Moves: Sonic Boom, Sand Attack, Feint Attack, Sand Tomb, Mud-Slap, Bide, Bulldoze, Rock Slide, Supersonic, Screech, Dragon Breath, Earth Power, Sandstorm, Dragon Tail, Hyper Beam, Dragon Claw

When it needs a hiding place, Flygon beats its wings rapidly to create a sandstorm. This Pokémon is known as "The Desert Spirit."

Trapinch ➡ Vibrava ➡ Flygon

FOONGUS

Mushroom Pokémon

How to say it: FOON-gus

Height: 0' 08"   **Weight:** 2.2 lbs.

Possible Moves: Absorb, Growth, Astonish, Bide, Mega Drain, Ingrain, Feint Attack, Sweet Scent, Giga Drain, Toxic, Synthesis, Clear Smog, Solar Beam, Rage Powder, Spore

Foongus uses its deceptive Poké Ball pattern to lure people or Pokémon close. Then it attacks with poison spores.

Foongus   Amoonguss

GABITE
Cave Pokémon

TYPE:
DRAGON-GROUND

How to say it: gab-BITE

Height: 4' 07"
Weight: 123.5 lbs.

Possible Moves: Tackle, Sand Attack, Dragon Rage, Sandstorm, Take Down, Sand Tomb, Dual Chop, Slash, Dragon Claw, Dig, Dragon Rush

While digging to expand its nest, Gabite sometimes finds sparkly gems that then become part of its hoard.

Gible → Gabite → Garchomp → Mega Garchomp

GARBODOR
Trash Heap Pokémon

TYPE:
POISON

How to say it: gar-BOH-dur

Height: 6' 03"
Weight: 236.6 lbs.

Possible Moves: Pound, Poison Gas, Recycle, Toxic Spikes, Acid Spray, Double Slap, Sludge, Stockpile, Swallow, Body Slam, Sludge Bomb, Clear Smog, Toxic, Amnesia, Belch, Gunk Shot, Explosion

Garbodor wraps its long left arm around an opponent to bring it within range of its poisonous breath. It creates new kinds of poison by eating garbage.

Trubbish → Garbodor

GARCHOMP

Mach Pokémon

How to say it: gar-CHOMP

Height: 6' 03"
Weight: 209.4 lbs.

Possible Moves: Fire Fang, Tackle, Sand Attack, Dragon Rage, Sandstorm, Take Down, Sand Tomb, Dual Chop, Slash, Dragon Claw, Dig, Crunch, Dragon Rush

Garchomp can fly faster than the speed of sound. When it assumes a streamlined position for flight, it looks like a fighter jet.

TYPE:
DRAGON-GROUND

MEGA GARCHOMP

Mach Pokémon

Height: 6' 03"
Weight: 209.4 lbs.

TYPE:
DRAGON-GROUND

Gible → Gabite → Garchomp → Mega Garchomp

GASTLY
Gas Pokémon

How to say it: GAST-lee

Height: 4' 03" **Weight:** 0.2 lbs.

Possible Moves: Hypnosis, Lick, Spite, Mean Look, Curse, Night Shade, Confuse Ray, Sucker Punch, Payback, Shadow Ball, Dream Eater, Dark Pulse, Destiny Bond, Hex, Nightmare

Gastly's body is formed of poisonous gases. It can envelop opponents in its gaseous body to cut off their air.

TYPE:
GHOST-
POISON

Gastly   Haunter   Gengar   Mega Gengar

GENGAR
Shadow Pokémon

How to say it: GHEN-gar

Height: 4' 11"
Weight: 89.3 lbs.

Possible Moves: Hypnosis, Lick, Spite, Mean Look, Curse, Night Shade, Confuse Ray, Sucker Punch, Shadow Punch, Payback, Shadow Ball, Dream Eater, Dark Pulse, Destiny Bond, Hex, Nightmare

Gengar stalks the shadows at night, absorbing heat and creating a creepy chill in the air. A sudden shiver could mean a Gengar is hiding nearby.

TYPE:
GHOST-POISON

MEGA GENGAR
Shadow Pokémon

Height: 4' 07"
Weight: 89.3 lbs.

TYPE:
GHOST-POISON

Gastly   Haunter   Gengar   Mega Gengar

GEODUDE
Rock Pokémon

TYPE:
ROCK-
GROUND

How to say it: JEE-oh-dude

Height: 1' 04"   **Weight:** 44.1 lbs.

Possible Moves: Tackle, Defense Curl, Mud Sport, Rock Polish, Rollout, Magnitude, Rock Throw, Rock Blast, Smack Down, Self-Destruct, Bulldoze, Stealth Rock, Earthquake, Explosion, Double-Edge, Stone Edge

Geodude look just like rocks when they aren't moving. They hold contests to see which one has the hardest surface by crashing into each other.

Geodude   Graveler   Golem

GIBLE
Land Shark Pokémon

TYPE:
DRAGON-
GROUND

How to say it: GIB-bull

Height: 2' 04"   **Weight:** 45.2 lbs.

Possible Moves: Tackle, Sand Attack, Dragon Rage, Sandstorm, Take Down, Sand Tomb, Slash, Dragon Claw, Dig, Dragon Rush

Gible dig holes in the walls of warm caves to make their nests. Don't get too close, or they might pounce!

Gible   Gabite   Garchomp   Mega Garchomp

GLIGAR
Fly Scorpion Pokémon

How to say it: GLY-gar

Height: 3' 07"
Weight: 142.9 lbs.

TYPE: GROUND-FLYING

Possible Moves: Poison Sting, Sand Attack, Harden, Knock Off, Quick Attack, Fury Cutter, Feint Attack, Acrobatics, Slash, U-turn, Screech, X-Scissor, Sky Uppercut, Swords Dance, Guillotine

Clinging to the side of a cliff, Gligar has the high ground—and the element of surprise. It strikes from above, grabbing on to its startled opponent's face.

Gligar   Gliscor

GLISCOR
Fang Scorpion Pokémon

How to say it: GLY-score

Height: 6' 07"   **Weight:** 93.7 lbs.

Possible Moves: Guillotine, Thunder Fang, Ice Fang, Fire Fang, Poison Jab, Sand Attack, Harden, Knock Off, Quick Attack, Fury Cutter, Feint Attack, Acrobatics, Night Slash, U-turn, Screech, X-Scissor, Sky Uppercut, Swords Dance

Gliscor hangs upside down from trees, watching for its chance to attack. At the right moment, it silently swoops, with its long tail ready to seize its opponent.

TYPE: GROUND-FLYING

Gligar   Gliscor

GOLEM
Megaton Pokémon

TYPE:
ROCK-GROUND

How to say it: GO-lum

Height: 4' 07"
Weight: 661.4 lbs.

Possible Moves: Heavy Slam, Tackle, Defense Curl, Mud Sport, Rock Polish, Steamroller, Magnitude, Rock Throw, Rock Blast, Smack Down, Self-Destruct, Bulldoze, Stealth Rock, Earthquake, Explosion, Double-Edge, Stone Edge

When Golem roll down mountains, they leave deep grooves in the rock. Their boulderlike surface protects them from anything, even a dynamite blast.

Geodude ➡ Graveler ➡ Golem

GOODRA
Dragon Pokémon

TYPE:
DRAGON

How to say it: GOO-druh

Height: 6' 07"
Weight: 331.8 lbs.

Possible Moves: Outrage, Feint, Tackle, Bubble, Absorb, Protect, Bide, Dragon Breath, Rain Dance, Flail, Body Slam, Muddy Water, Dragon Pulse, Aqua Tail, Power Whip

The affectionate Goodra just loves to give its Trainer a big hug! Unfortunately, its hugs leave the recipient covered in goo.

Goomy ➡ Sliggoo ➡ Goodra

GOOMY

Soft Tissue Pokémon

How to say it: GOO-mee

Height: 1' 00"   **Weight:** 6.2 lbs.

Possible Moves: Tackle, Bubble, Absorb, Protect, Bide, Dragon Breath, Rain Dance, Flail, Body Slam, Muddy Water, Dragon Pulse

The slippery membrane that covers Goomy's body deflects the fists and feet of its attackers. To keep itself from drying out, it stays away from the sun.

TYPE: DRAGON

Goomy   Sliggoo   Goodra

GOTHITA

Fixation Pokémon

TYPE: PSYCHIC

How to say it: GAH-THEE-tah

Height: 1' 04"   **Weight:** 12.8 lbs.

Possible Moves: Pound, Confusion, Tickle, Play Nice, Fake Tears, Double Slap, Psybeam, Embargo, Feint Attack, Psyshock, Flatter, Future Sight, Heal Block, Psychic, Telekinesis, Charm, Magic Room

Gothita's wide eyes are always fixed on something. It seems when they stare like that, they're seeing what others cannot.

Gothita   Gothorita   Gothitelle

GOTHITELLE
Astral Body Pokémon

How to say it: GAH-thih-tell

Height: 4' 11"
Weight: 97.0 lbs.

Possible Moves: Pound, Confusion, Tickle, Play Nice, Fake Tears, Double Slap, Psybeam, Embargo, Feint Attack, Psyshock, Flatter, Future Sight, Heal Block, Psychic, Telekinesis, Charm, Magic Room

Gothitelle observes the stars to predict the future. It sometimes distorts the air around itself to reveal faraway constellations.

TYPE: PSYCHIC

Gothita → Gothorita → Gothitelle

GOTHORITA
Manipulate Pokémon

How to say it: GAH-thoh-REE-tah

Height: 2' 04"　**Weight:** 39.7 lbs.

Possible Moves: Pound, Confusion, Tickle, Play Nice, Fake Tears, Double Slap, Psybeam, Embargo, Feint Attack, Psyshock, Flatter, Future Sight, Heal Block, Psychic, Telekinesis, Charm, Magic Room

Gothorita draw their power from starlight. On starry nights, they can make stones float and control people's movements with their enhanced psychic power.

TYPE: PSYCHIC

Gothita → Gothorita → Gothitelle

GOURGEIST
Pumpkin Pokémon

TYPE: GHOST-GRASS

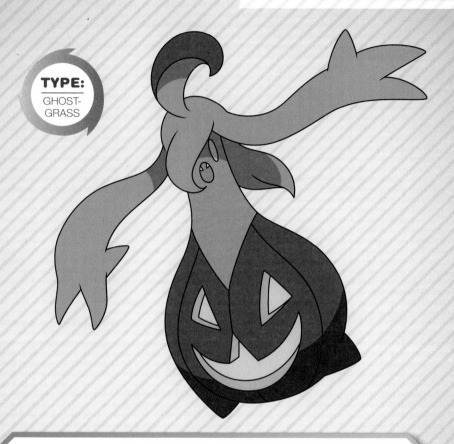

How to say it: GORE-guyst

Height: 2' 11"   **Weight:** 27.6 lbs.

Possible Moves: Explosion, Phantom Force, Trick, Astonish, Confuse Ray, Scary Face, Trick-or-Treat, Worry Seed, Razor Leaf, Leech Seed, Bullet Seed, Shadow Sneak, Shadow Ball, Pain Split, Seed Bomb

During the new moon, the eerie song of the Gourgeist echoes through town, bringing woe to anyone who hears it.

Pumpkaboo   ➡   Gourgeist

GRAVELER
Rock Pokémon

How to say it: GRAV-el-ler

Height: 3' 03"   **Weight:** 231.5 lbs.

Possible Moves: Tackle, Defense Curl, Mud Sport, Rock Polish, Rollout, Magnitude, Rock Throw, Rock Blast, Smack Down, Self-Destruct, Bulldoze, Stealth Rock, Earthquake, Explosion, Double-Edge, Stone Edge

Graveler move by rolling downhill. They'll roll right over anything that gets in their way, and they don't even notice if bits of themselves break off in the process.

TYPE:
ROCK-
GROUND

Geodude   Graveler   Golem

GURDURR
Muscular Pokémon

TYPE:
FIGHTING

How to say it: GUR-dur

Height: 3' 11"   **Weight:** 88.2 lbs.

Possible Moves: Pound, Leer, Focus Energy, Bide, Low Kick, Rock Throw, Wake-Up Slap, Chip Away, Bulk Up, Rock Slide, Dynamic Punch, Scary Face, Hammer Arm, Stone Edge, Focus Punch, Superpower

With its strong muscles, Gurdurr can wield its steel beam with ease in battle. It's so sturdy that a whole team of wrestlers couldn't knock it down.

Timburr   Gurdurr   Conkeldurr

HAUNTER

Gas Pokémon

How to say it: HAUNT-ur

Height: 5' 03"
Weight: 0.2 lbs.

Possible Moves: Hypnosis, Lick, Spite, Mean Look, Curse, Night Shade, Confuse Ray, Sucker Punch, Shadow Punch, Payback, Shadow Ball, Dream Eater, Dark Pulse, Destiny Bond, Hex, Nightmare

Haunter lurks in dark places, waiting for people to pass by so it can steal their life force with a ghostly lick.

Gastly   Haunter   Gengar   Mega Gengar

TYPE:
GHOST-POISON

HEATMOR

Anteater Pokémon

TYPE:
FIRE

How to say it: HEET-mohr

Height: 4' 07"
Weight: 127.9 lbs.

Possible Moves: Inferno, Hone Claws, Tackle, Incinerate, Lick, Odor Sleuth, Bind, Fire Spin, Fury Swipes, Snatch, Flame Burst, Bug Bite, Slash, Amnesia, Flamethrower, Stockpile, Spit Up, Swallow

Heatmor can control the flame from its mouth like a tongue, and the fire is so hot that it can melt through steel. Heatmor and Durant are natural enemies.

Does not evolve

HONCHKROW

Big Boss Pokémon

How to say it: HONCH-krow

Height: 2' 11"   **Weight:** 60.2 lbs.

Possible Moves: Night Slash, Sucker Punch, Astonish, Pursuit, Haze, Wing Attack, Swagger, Nasty Plot, Foul Play, Quash, Dark Pulse

When Honchkrow cries out in its deep voice, several Murkrow will appear to answer the call. Honchkrow is most active after dark.

TYPE: DARK-FIGHTING

Murkrow   Honchkrow

HOOTHOOT

Owl Pokémon

How to say it: HOOT-HOOT

Height: 2' 04"   **Weight:** 46.7 lbs.

Possible Moves: Tackle, Growl, Foresight, Hypnosis, Peck, Uproar, Reflect, Confusion, Echoed Voice, Take Down, Air Slash, Zen Headbutt, Synchronoise, Extrasensory, Psycho Shift, Roost, Dream Eater

Although Hoothoot does have two feet, it's rare to see them both at the same time. Usually it balances on one foot while keeping the other tucked up into its feathers.

TYPE: NORMAL-FLYING

Hoothoot   Noctowl

HYDREIGON
Brutal Pokémon

How to say it: hy-DRY-gahn

Height: 5' 11"
Weight: 352.7 lbs.

Possible Moves: Outrage, Hyper Voice, Tri Attack, Dragon Rage, Focus Energy, Bite, Headbutt, Dragon Breath, Roar, Crunch, Slam, Dragon Pulse, Work Up, Dragon Rush, Body Slam, Scary Face

The smaller heads on Hydreigon's arms don't have brains, but they can still eat. Any movement within its line of sight will be greeted with a frightening attack.

Deino   Zweilous   Hydreigon

IGGLYBUFF
Balloon Pokémon

TYPE:
NORMAL-FAIRY

How to say it: IG-lee-buff

Height: 1' 00"   **Weight:** 2.2 lbs.

Possible Moves: Sing, Charm, Defense Curl, Pound, Sweet Kiss, Copycat

Igglybuff has very short legs, so instead of walking, it usually moves by bouncing. If it gets off-balance, it starts rolling and can't stop.

Igglybuff   Jigglypuff   Wigglytuff

JIGGLYPUFF
Balloon Pokémon

TYPE:
NORMAL-
FAIRY

How to say it: JIG-lee-puff

Height: 1' 08"
Weight: 12.1 lbs.

Possible Moves: Sing, Defense Curl, Pound, Play Nice, Disable, Round, Rollout, Double Slap, Rest, Body Slam, Gyro Ball, Wake-Up Slap, Mimic, Hyper Voice, Disarming Voice, Double-Edge

Jigglypuff is known for its soothing lullabies. It can inflate its round body, which gives it enough air to keep singing until everyone falls asleep.

Igglybuff   Jigglypuff   Wigglytuff

JYNX
Human Shape Pokémon

TYPE:
ICE-
PSYCHIC

How to say it: JINX

Height: 4' 07"
Weight: 89.5 lbs.

Possible Moves: Draining Kiss, Perish Song, Pound, Lick, Lovely Kiss, Powder Snow, Double Slap, Ice Punch, Heart Stamp, Mean Look, Fake Tears, Wake-Up Slap, Avalanche, Body Slam, Wring Out, Blizzard

Jynx talk to each other in a complex language that resembles human speech. Researchers are still trying to figure out what they're saying.

Smoochum   Jynx

KARRABLAST

Clamping Pokémon

How to say it: KAIR-ruh-blast

Height: 1' 08"
Weight: 13.0 lbs.

Possible Moves: Peck, Leer, Endure, Fury Cutter, Fury Attack, Headbutt, False Swipe, Bug Buzz, Slash, Take Down, Scary Face, X-Scissor, Flail, Swords Dance, Double-Edge

Karrablast often attack Shelmet, trying to steal their shells. When electrical energy envelops them at the same time, they both evolve.

TYPE:
BUG

Karrablast ▶ **Escavalier**

KLEFKI

Key Ring Pokémon

TYPE:
STEEL-
FAIRY

How to say it: KLEF-key

Height: 0' 08"
Weight: 6.6 lbs.

Possible Moves: Fairy Lock, Tackle, Fairy Wind, Astonish, Metal Sound, Spikes, Draining Kiss, Crafty Shield, Foul Play, Torment, Mirror Shot, Imprison, Recycle, Play Rough, Magic Room, Heal Block

To keep valuables locked up tight, give the key to a Klefki. This Pokémon loves to collect keys, and it will guard its collection with all its might.

Does not evolve

LAIRON

Iron Armor Pokémon

TYPE:
STEEL-ROCK

How to say it: LAIR-ron

Height: 2' 11"
Weight: 264.6 lbs.

Possible Moves: Tackle, Harden, Mud-Slap, Headbutt, Metal Claw, Iron Defense, Roar, Take Down, Iron Head, Protect, Metal Sound, Iron Tail, Autotomize, Heavy Slam, Double-Edge, Metal Burst

Lairon's favorite food is iron ore. In battles over territory, these Pokémon smash into one another with their steel bodies.

Aron ➜ Lairon ➜ Aggron ➜ Mega Aggron

LAMPENT

Lamp Pokémon

How to say it: LAM-pent

Height: 2' 00"   **Weight:** 28.7 lbs.

Possible Moves: Ember, Astonish, Minimize, Smog, Fire Spin, Confuse Ray, Night Shade, Will-O-Wisp, Flame Burst, Imprison, Hex, Memento, Inferno, Curse, Shadow Ball, Pain Split, Overheat

Lampent tends to lurk grimly around hospitals, waiting for someone to take a bad turn so it can absorb the departing spirit. The stolen spirits keep its fire burning.

TYPE:
GHOST-FIRE

Litwick ➜ Lampent ➜ Chandelure

LARVITAR
Rock Skin Pokémon

How to say it: LAR-vuh-tar

Height: 2' 00" **Weight:** 158.7 lbs.

Possible Moves: Bite, Leer, Sandstorm, Screech, Chip Away, Rock Slide, Scary Face, Thrash, Dark Pulse, Payback, Crunch, Earthquake, Stone Edge, Hyper Beam

Larvitar uses soil as food, and its appetite is so great that it could eat an entire mountain. Afterward, it sleeps and grows.

Larvitar → Pupitar → Tyranitar → Mega Tyranitar

TYPE:
ROCK-GROUND

LICKILICKY
Licking Pokémon

TYPE:
NORMAL

How to say it: LICK-ee-LICK-ee

Height: 5' 07"
Weight: 308.6 lbs.

Possible Moves: Wring Out, Power Whip, Lick, Supersonic, Defense Curl, Knock Off, Wrap, Stomp, Disable, Slam, Rollout, Chip Away, Me First, Refresh, Screech, Gyro Ball

Lickilicky can make its long tongue even longer, stretching it out to wrap around food or foe. Its drool causes a lasting numbness.

Lickitung → Lickilicky

LICKITUNG
Licking Pokémon

TYPE: NORMAL

How to say it: LICK-it-tung

Height: 3' 11"
Weight: 144.4 lbs.

Possible Moves: Lick, Supersonic, Defense Curl, Knock Off, Wrap, Stomp, Disable, Slam, Rollout, Chip Away, Me First, Refresh, Screech, Power Whip, Wring Out

Lickitung's sticky tongue is twice as long as its body. It uses this long, mobile tongue as an extra appendage.

Lickitung ➡ **Lickilicky**

LIEPARD
Cruel Pokémon

TYPE: DARK

How to say it: LY-purd

Height: 3' 07"   **Weight:** 82.7 lbs.

Possible Moves: Scratch, Growl, Assist, Sand Attack, Fury Swipes, Pursuit, Torment, Fake Out, Hone Claws, Assurance, Slash, Taunt, Night Slash, Snatch, Nasty Plot, Sucker Punch, Play Rough

Elegant and swift, Liepard can move through the night without a sound. It uses this stealth to execute sneak attacks.

Purrloin   **Liepard**

LITWICK
Candle Pokémon

TYPE: GHOST-FIRE

How to say it: LIT-wik

Height: 1' 00"　**Weight:** 6.8 lbs.

Possible Moves: Ember, Astonish, Minimize, Smog, Fire Spin, Confuse Ray, Night Shade, Will-O-Wisp, Flame Burst, Imprison, Hex, Memento, Inferno, Curse, Shadow Ball, Pain Split, Overheat

Litwick pretends to guide people and Pokémon with its light, but following it is a bad idea. The ghostly flame absorbs life energy for use as fuel.

Litwick　Lampent　Chandelure

LOMBRE
Jolly Pokémon

TYPE: WATER-GRASS

How to say it: LOM-brey

Height: 3' 11"　**Weight:** 71.6 lbs.

Possible Moves: Astonish, Growl, Absorb, Nature Power, Fake Out, Fury Swipes, Water Sport, Bubble Beam, Zen Headbutt, Uproar, Hydro Pump

When Lombre spots someone fishing from the sunny shores where it makes its home, it often gives the line a playful tug.

Lotad　Lombre　Ludicolo

LOTAD
Water Weed Pokémon

TYPE:
WATER-GRASS

How to say it: LOW-tad

Height: 1' 08"   **Weight:** 5.7 lbs.

Possible Moves: Astonish, Growl, Absorb, Nature Power, Mist, Natural Gift, Mega Drain, Bubble Beam, Zen Headbutt, Rain Dance, Energy Ball

The large, flat leaf on Lotad's back makes an excellent ferry for smaller Pokémon who need to cross water.

Lotad   Lombre   Ludicolo

LUDICOLO
Carefree Pokémon

TYPE:
WATER-GRASS

How to say it: LOO-dee-KO-low

Height: 4' 11"
Weight: 121.3 lbs.

Possible Moves: Astonish, Growl, Mega Drain, Nature Power

Ludicolo just can't help leaping into a joyful dance when it hears a festive tune. Rhythmic music fills it with energy.

Lotad   Lombre   Ludicolo

MAGCARGO
Lava Pokémon

How to say it: mag-CAR-go

Height: 2' 07"
Weight: 121.3 lbs.

TYPE:
FIRE-
ROCK

Possible Moves: Earth Power, Yawn, Smog, Ember, Rock Throw, Harden, Recover, Flame Burst, Ancient Power, Amnesia, Lava Plume, Shell Smash, Rock Slide, Body Slam, Flamethrower

Magcargo's body is so hot that its brittle shell sometimes bursts into flame, giving off waves of intense heat.

Slugma → Magcargo

MAGNEMITE
Magnet Pokémon

How to say it: MAG-nuh-mite

Height: 1' 00"   **Weight:** 13.2 lbs.

TYPE:
ELECTRIC-
STEEL

Possible Moves: Tackle, Supersonic, Thunder Shock, Sonic Boom, Thunder Wave, Magnet Bomb, Spark, Mirror Shot, Metal Sound, Electro Ball, Flash Cannon, Screech, Discharge, Lock-On, Magnet Rise, Gyro Ball, Zap Cannon

From the units at its sides, Magnemite generates an antigravity field to keep itself afloat. The units can also unleash electrical attacks.

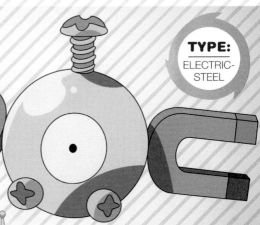

Magnemite → Magneton → Magnezone

MAGNETON
Magnet Pokémon

How to say it: MAG-nuh-ton

Height: 3' 03" **Weight:** 132.3 lbs.

Possible Moves: Zap Cannon, Tri Attack, Tackle, Supersonic, Thunder Shock, Sonic Boom, Electric Terrain, Thunder Wave, Magnet Bomb, Spark, Mirror Shot, Metal Sound, Electro Ball, Flash Cannon, Screech, Discharge, Lock-On, Magnet Rise, Gyro Ball

Several Magnemite link together to form a single Magneton. When Magneton is nearby, the magnetic waves it gives off jumble radio signals and raise the surrounding temperature.

TYPE:
ELECTRIC-
STEEL

Magnemite   Magneton   Magnezone

MAGNEZONE
Magnet Area Pokémon

How to say it: MAG-nuh-zone

Height: 3' 11" **Weight:** 396.8 lbs.

Possible Moves: Zap Cannon, Magnetic Flux, Mirror Coat, Barrier, Tackle, Supersonic, Sonic Boom, Thunder Shock, Electric Terrain, Thunder Wave, Magnet Bomb, Spark, Mirror Shot, Metal Sound, Electro Ball, Flash Cannon, Screech, Discharge, Lock-On, Magnet Rise, Gyro Ball

Magnezone give off a strong magnetic field that they can't always control. Sometimes they attract one another by accident and stick so tightly that they have trouble separating.

TYPE:
ELECTRIC-
STEEL

Magnemite   Magneton   Magnezone

MAMOSWINE

Twin Tusk Pokémon

TYPE:
ICE-
GROUND

How to say it: MAM-oh-swine

Height: 8' 02"   **Weight:** 641.5 lbs.

Possible Moves: Scary Face, Ancient Power, Peck, Odor Sleuth, Mud Sport, Powder Snow, Mud-Slap, Endure, Mud Bomb, Hail, Ice Fang, Take Down, Double Hit, Mist, Thrash, Earthquake, Blizzard

Mamoswine have been around since the last ice age, but the warmer climate reduced their population. Their huge twin tusks are formed of ice.

Swinub   Piloswine   Mamoswine

MEWTWO
Genetic Pokémon

TYPE: PSYCHIC

How to say it: MUE-too

Height: 6' 07"　**Weight:** 269.0 lbs.

Possible Moves: Confusion, Disable, Barrier, Swift, Future Sight, Psych Up, Miracle Eye, Mist, Psycho Cut, Amnesia, Power Swap, Guard Swap, Psychic, Me First, Recover, Safeguard, Aura Sphere, Psystrike

This incredibly powerful Pokémon was created as part of a brutal scientific experiment involving genetic splicing. As a result, Mewtwo is extremely savage and dangerous.

MEGA MEWTWO X
Genetic Pokémon

Height: 7' 07"
Weight: 280.0 lbs.

TYPE: PSYCHIC-FIGHTING

MEGA MEWTWO Y
Genetic Pokémon

Height: 4' 11"
Weight: 72.8 lbs.

TYPE: PSYCHIC

Mega Mewtwo X

Mewtwo

Mega Mewtwo Y

MIGHTYENA
Bite Pokémon

How to say it: MY-tee-EH-nah

Height: 3' 03"
Weight: 81.6 lbs.

Possible Moves: Crunch, Tackle, Howl, Sand Attack, Bite, Howl, Odor Sleuth, Roar, Swagger, Assurance, Scary Face, Taunt, Embargo, Take Down, Thief, Sucker Punch

TYPE: DARK

In the wild, Mightyena hunt in packs and work together to take down an opponent. Skilled Trainers find that this ancient instinct makes them obedient partners.

Poochyena   Mightyena

MURKROW
Darkness Pokémon

How to say it: MUR-crow

Height: 1' 08"
Weight: 4.6 lbs.

Possible Moves: Peck, Astonish, Pursuit, Haze, Wing Attack, Night Shade, Assurance, Taunt, Feint Attack, Mean Look, Foul Play, Tailwind, Sucker Punch, Torment, Quash

TYPE: DARK-FLYING

Some people believe that if you see a Murkrow at night, bad luck will follow. This Pokémon is attracted to shiny objects and often swipes them to add to its hoard.

Murkrow   Honchkrow

NOCTOWL
Owl Pokémon

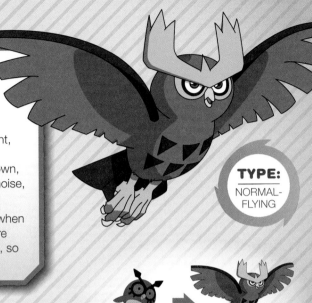

How to say it: NAHK-towl

Height: 5' 03"
Weight: 89.9 lbs.

Possible Moves: Dream Eater, Sky Attack, Tackle, Growl, Foresight, Hypnosis, Peck, Uproar, Reflect, Confusion, Echoed Voice, Take Down, Air Slash, Zen Headbutt, Synchronoise, Extrasensory, Psycho Shift, Roost

Noctowl turns its head backward when it needs to concentrate. Its eyes are designed to focus the faintest light, so it can see in near-total darkness.

TYPE:
NORMAL-FLYING

Hoothoot → Noctowl

NOIBAT
Sound Wave Pokémon

TYPE:
FLYING-DRAGON

How to say it: NOY-bat

Height: 1' 08"
Weight: 17.6 lbs.

Possible Moves: Screech, Supersonic, Tackle, Leech Life, Gust, Bite, Wing Attack, Agility, Air Cutter, Roost, Razor Wind, Tailwind, Whirlwind, Super Fang, Air Slash, Hurricane

Noibat live in lightless caves and communicate with ultrasonic waves emitted from their ears. These waves can make a strong man dizzy.

Noibat → Noivern

NOIVERN
Sound Wave Pokémon

How to say it: NOY-vurn

Height: 4' 11"   **Weight:** 187.4 lbs.

Possible Moves: Moonlight, Boomburst, Dragon Pulse, Hurricane, Screech, Supersonic, Tackle, Leech Life, Gust, Bite, Wing Attack, Agility, Air Cutter, Roost, Razor Wind, Tailwind, Whirlwind, Super Fang, Air Slash

Noivern are masters when it comes to battling in the dark. The ultrasonic waves they release from their ears are powerful enough to crush a boulder.

TYPE:
FLYING-DRAGON

Noibat   Noivern

PATRAT
Scout Pokémon

How to say it: pat-RAT

Height: 1' 08"   **Weight:** 25.6 lbs.

Possible Moves: Tackle, Leer, Bite, Bide, Detect, Sand Attack, Crunch, Hypnosis, Super Fang, After You, Work Up, Hyper Fang, Mean Look, Baton Pass, Slam

Wary and cautious, Patrat are very serious about their job as lookouts. They store food in their cheeks so they don't have to leave their posts.

TYPE:
NORMAL

Patrat   Watchog

PAWNIARD
Sharp Blade Pokémon

How to say it: PAWN-yard

Height: 1' 08"
Weight: 22.5 lbs.

Possible Moves: Scratch, Leer, Fury Cutter, Torment, Feint Attack, Scary Face, Metal Claw, Slash, Assurance, Metal Sound, Embargo, Iron Defense, Night Slash, Iron Head, Swords Dance, Guillotine

Pawniard's body is covered in blades, which it keeps sharp by polishing them after battle. Even when hurt, it's a relentless hunter.

TYPE: DARK-STEEL

Pawniard ➡ Bisharp

PHANTUMP
Stump Pokémon

How to say it: FAN-tump

Height: 1' 04"
Weight: 15.4 lbs.

Possible Moves: Tackle, Confuse Ray, Astonish, Growth, Ingrain, Feint Attack, Leech Seed, Curse, Will-O-Wisp, Forest's Curse, Destiny Bond, Phantom Force, Wood Hammer, Horn Leech

It is said that when the spirits of wandering children inhabit old tree stumps, these Pokémon are created. Phantump dwell in lonely forests, far away from people.

TYPE: GHOST-GRASS

Phantump ➡ Trevenant

PILOSWINE
Swine Pokémon

How to say it: PILE-oh-swine

Height: 3' 07"
Weight: 123.0 lbs.

Possible Moves: Ancient Power, Peck, Odor Sleuth, Mud Sport, Powder Snow, Mud-Slap, Endure, Mud Bomb, Icy Wind, Ice Fang, Take Down, Fury Attack, Mist, Thrash, Earthquake, Blizzard, Amnesia

TYPE: ICE-GROUND

Piloswine can't see very well because the long hair that protects it from the cold also covers its eyes. The rough surface of its hooves grips the ice to keep it from slipping.

Swinub Piloswine Mamoswine

POLITOED
Frog Pokémon

How to say it: PAUL-lee-TOED

Height: 3' 07"   **Weight:** 74.7 lbs.

Possible Moves: Bubble Beam, Hypnosis, Double Slap, Perish Song, Swagger, Bounce, Hyper Voice

It sounds an echoing cry to summon Poliwag and Poliwhirl from anywhere within earshot. When more than two Politoed gather together, they join voices in a bellowing song.

TYPE: WATER

Poliwag Poliwhirl Politoed

POLIWAG
Tadpole Pokémon

TYPE: WATER

How to say it: PAUL-lee-wag

Height: 2' 00"
Weight: 27.3 lbs.

Possible Moves: Water Sport, Water Gun, Hypnosis, Bubble, Double Slap, Rain Dance, Body Slam, Bubble Beam, Mud Shot, Belly Drum, Wake-Up Slap, Hydro Pump, Mud Bomb

The direction of the spiral pattern on Poliwag's belly is different depending on where it lives. It can get around much more easily in the water than on land.

Poliwag → Poliwhirl → Poliwrath / Politoed

POLIWHIRL
Tadpole Pokémon

TYPE: WATER

How to say it: PAUL-lee-wirl

Height: 3' 03"   **Weight:** 44.1 lbs.

Possible Moves: Water Sport, Water Gun, Hypnosis, Bubble, Double Slap, Rain Dance, Body Slam, Bubble Beam, Mud Shot, Belly Drum, Wake-Up Slap, Hydro Pump, Mud Bomb

Poliwhirl sweats profusely when on land to keep its skin moist. Though its legs have developed to make walking easier, it prefers to swim.

Poliwag → Poliwhirl → Poliwrath / Politoed

POLIWRATH
Tadpole Pokémon

How to say it: PAUL-lee-rath

Height: 4' 03" **Weight:** 119.0 lbs.

Possible Moves: Circle Throw, Bubble Beam, Hypnosis, Double Slap, Submission, Dynamic Punch, Mind Reader

A strong and tireless swimmer, Poliwrath is tough enough to withstand the constant waves and currents of the ocean.

TYPE:
WATER-
FIGHTING

Poliwag Poliwhirl Poliwrath

POOCHYENA
Bite Pokémon

How to say it: POO-chee-EH-nah

Height: 1' 08"
Weight: 30.0 lbs.

Possible Moves: Tackle, Howl, Sand Attack, Bite, Odor Sleuth, Roar, Swagger, Assurance, Scary Face, Taunt, Embargo, Take Down, Sucker Punch, Crunch

An unrelenting tracker, Poochyena can use scent to stay on the trail of a fleeing opponent long after it disappears from view.

TYPE:
DARK

Poochyena Mightyena

PUMPKABOO
Pumpkin Pokémon

TYPE:
GHOST-
GRASS

How to say it: PUMP-kuh-boo

Height: 1' 04"   **Weight:** 11.0 lbs.

Possible Moves: Trick, Astonish, Confuse Ray, Scary Face, Trick-or-Treat, Worry Seed, Razor Leaf, Leech Seed, Bullet Seed, Shadow Sneak, Shadow Ball, Pain Split, Seed Bomb

The nocturnal Pumpkaboo tends to get restless as darkness falls. Stories say it serves as a guide for wandering spirits, leading them through the night to find their true home.

Pumpkaboo   Gourgeist

PUPITAR
Hard Shell Pokémon

How to say it: PUE-puh-tar

Height: 3' 11"   **Weight:** 335.1 lbs.

Possible Moves: Bite, Leer, Sandstorm, Screech, Chip Away, Rock Slide, Scary Face, Thrash, Dark Pulse, Payback, Crunch, Earthquake, Stone Edge, Hyper Beam

Pupitar can pressurize gases inside its rock-hard shell and use them for propulsion.

TYPE:
ROCK-GROUND

Larvitar   **Pupitar**   **Tyranitar**   **Mega Tyranitar**

PURRLOIN
Devious Pokémon

How to say it: PUR-loyn

Height: 1' 04"   **Weight:** 22.3 lbs.

Possible Moves: Scratch, Growl, Assist, Sand Attack, Fury Swipes, Pursuit, Torment, Fake Out, Hone Claws, Assurance, Slash, Captivate, Night Slash, Snatch, Nasty Plot, Sucker Punch, Play Rough

Purrloin acts cute and innocent to trick people into trusting it. Then it steals their stuff.

Purrloin   **Liepard**

TYPE:
DARK

QUAGSIRE
Water Fish Pokémon

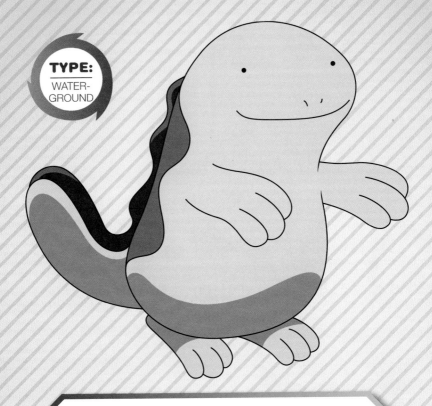

TYPE:
WATER-
GROUND

How to say it: KWAG-sire

Height: 4' 07"   **Weight:** 165.3 lbs.

Possible Moves: Water Gun, Tail Whip, Mud Sport, Mud Shot, Slam, Mud Bomb, Amnesia, Yawn, Earthquake, Rain Dance, Mist, Haze, Muddy Water

The laid-back Quagsire often bumps into boats as it swims slowly through the river. Sometimes it lounges on the riverbed and waits for food to float by.

Wooper   Quagsire

TYPE: ELECTRIC-GHOST

How to say it: ROW-tom

Height: 1' 00"
Weight: 0.7 lbs.

Possible Moves: Discharge, Charge, Trick, Astonish, Thunder Wave, Thunder Shock, Confuse Ray, Uproar, Double Team, Shock Wave, Ominous Wind, Substitute, Electro Ball, Hex

Scientists are conducting ongoing research on Rotom, which shows potential as a power source. Sometimes it sneaks into electrical appliances and causes trouble.

Frost Forme

Heat Forme

Fan Forme

Wash Forme

Mow Forme

Does not evolve

SANDSHREW
Mouse Pokémon

TYPE: GROUND

How to say it: SAND-shroo

Height: 2' 00"
Weight: 26.5 lbs.

Possible Moves: Scratch, Defense Curl, Sand Attack, Poison Sting, Rollout, Rapid Spin, Swift, Fury Cutter, Magnitude, Fury Swipes, Sand Tomb, Slash, Dig, Gyro Ball, Swords Dance, Sandstorm, Earthquake

Sandshrew can roll up into a ball to protect its soft belly. It lives underground in arid lands and doesn't like to get wet.

Sandshrew   Sandslash

SANDSLASH
Mouse Pokémon

How to say it: SAND-slash

Height: 3' 03"   **Weight:** 65.0 lbs.

Possible Moves: Scratch, Defense Curl, Sand Attack, Poison Sting, Rollout, Rapid Spin, Swift, Fury Cutter, Magnitude, Fury Swipes, Crush Claw, Sand Tomb, Slash, Dig, Gyro Ball, Swords Dance, Sandstorm, Earthquake

When Sandslash rolls into a ball, the spikes on its back stick out in all directions. These spikes sometimes break off if it digs too fast, but they grow back quickly.

TYPE: GROUND

Sandshrew   Sandslash

SCIZOR

Pincer Pokémon

How to say it: SI-zor

Height: 5' 11" **Weight:** 260.1 lbs.

Possible Moves: Feint, Bullet Punch, Quick Attack, Leer, Focus Energy, Pursuit, False Swipe, Agility, Metal Claw, Fury Cutter, Slash, Razor Wind, Iron Defense, X-Scissor, Night Slash, Double Hit, Iron Head, Swords Dance

Scizor's steely pincers can crush even the hardest objects. The eye patterns are meant to scare off enemies.

TYPE:
BUG-
STEEL

MEGA SCIZOR

Pincer Pokémon

Height: 6' 07"
Weight: 275.6 lbs.

TYPE:
BUG-
STEEL

Scyther Scizor Mega Scizor

SCYTHER
Mantis Pokémon

TYPE:
BUG-
FLYING

How to say it: SY-thur

Height: 4' 11"   **Weight:** 123.5 lbs.

Possible Moves: Vacuum Wave, Quick Attack, Leer, Focus Energy, Pursuit, False Swipe, Agility, Wing Attack, Fury Cutter, Slash, Razor Wind, Double Team, X-Scissor, Night Slash, Double Hit, Air Slash, Swords Dance, Feint

With the razor-sharp scythes on its arms, Scyther can unleash slashing attacks faster than the eye can see.

Scyther   Scizor   Mega Scizo

SHELMET
Snail Pokémon

TYPE:
BUG

How to say it: SHELL-mett

Height: 1' 04"   **Weight:** 17.0 lbs.

Possible Moves: Leech Life, Acid, Bide, Curse, Struggle Bug, Mega Drain, Yawn, Protect, Acid Armor, Giga Drain, Body Slam, Bug Buzz, Recover, Guard Swap, Final Gambit

Shelmet evolves when exposed to electricity, but only if Karrablast is nearby. It's unclear why this is the case.

Shelmet   Accelgor

SHUCKLE
Mold Pokémon

TYPE:
BUG-ROCK

How to say it: SHUCK-kull

Height: 2' 00"
Weight: 45.2 lbs.

Possible Moves: Sticky Web, Withdraw, Constrict, Bide, Rollout, Encore, Wrap, Struggle Bug, Safeguard, Rest, Rock Throw, Gastro Acid, Power Trick, Shell Smash, Rock Slide, Bug Bite, Power Split, Guard Split, Stone Edge

Shuckle keeps berries in its shell to eat them later. If it forgets, its movements eventually turn the berries into juice.

Does not evolve

SHUPPET
Puppet Pokémon

TYPE:
GHOST

How to say it: SHUP-pett

Height: 2' 00"
Weight: 5.1 lbs.

Possible Moves: Knock Off, Screech, Night Shade, Spite, Will-O-Wisp, Shadow Sneak, Curse, Feint Attack, Hex, Shadow Ball, Sucker Punch, Embargo, Snatch, Grudge, Trick

Shuppet are drawn to unpleasant emotions. They sometimes lurk outside houses at night to feed on the inhabitants' bad vibes.

Shuppet　　Banette　　Mega Banette

SKARMORY

Armor Bird Pokémon

TYPE:
STEEL-
FLYING

How to say it: SKAR-more-ree

Height: 5' 07"
Weight: 111.3 lbs.

Possible Moves: Leer, Peck,
Sand Attack, Swift, Agility, Fury Attack, Feint,
Air Cutter, Spikes, Metal Sound, Steel Wing,
Autotomize, Air Slash, Slash, Night Slash

Skarmory build their nests in thorny bushes, so
their wings toughen up from an early age. The
hard armor that covers them doesn't impair their
flying speed.

Does not evolve

SKORUPI

Scorpion Pokémon

TYPE:
POISON-
BUG

How to say it: skor-ROOP-ee

Height: 2' 07"   **Weight:** 26.5 lbs.

Possible Moves: Bite, Poison
Sting, Leer, Knock Off, Pin Missile,
Acupressure, Pursuit, Bug Bite, Poison
Fang, Venoshock, Hone Claws, Toxic
Spikes, Night Slash, Scary Face,
Crunch, Fell Stinger, Cross Poison

After burying itself in the sand, Skorupi
lurks in hiding. If an intruder gets
too close, it latches on with the
poisonous claws on its tail.

Skorupi   Drapion

SLIGGOO
Soft Tissue Pokémon

TYPE:
DRAGON

How to say it: SLIH-goo

Height: 2' 07"   **Weight:** 38.6 lbs.

Possible Moves: Tackle, Bubble, Absorb, Protect, Bide, Dragon Breath, Rain Dance, Flail, Body Slam, Muddy Water, Dragon Pulse

The four horns on Sliggoo's head are sense organs that allow the Pokémon to find its way by sound and smell.

Goomy   Sliggoo   Goodra

SLUGMA
Lava Pokémon

How to say it: SLUG-ma

Height: 2' 04"
Weight: 77.2 lbs.

Possible Moves: Yawn, Smog, Ember, Rock Throw, Harden, Recover, Flame Burst, Ancient Power, Amnesia, Lava Plume, Rock Slide, Body Slam, Flamethrower, Earth Power

In areas of volcanic activity, Slugma are regularly seen. They have to keep moving in search of heat, or the magma that makes up their bodies will harden.

TYPE:
FIRE

Slugma   Magcargo

SMOOCHUM
Kiss Pokémon

How to say it: SMOO-chum

Height: 1' 04"   **Weight:** 13.2 lbs.

Possible Moves: Pound, Lick, Sweet Kiss, Powder Snow, Confusion, Sing, Heart Stamp, Mean Look, Fake Tears, Lucky Chant, Avalanche, Psychic, Copycat, Perish Song, Blizzard

When Smoochum encounters an unfamiliar object, it conducts an examination using its sensitive lips. Its memory of what it does and doesn't like is also stored in its lips.

TYPE:
ICE-PSYCHIC

Smoochum   Jynx

SNEASEL
Sharp Claw Pokémon

How to say it: SNEE-zul

Height: 2' 11"   **Weight:** 61.7 lbs.

Possible Moves: Scratch, Leer, Taunt, Quick Attack, Feint Attack, Icy Wind, Fury Swipes, Agility, Metal Claw, Hone Claws, Beat Up, Screech, Slash, Snatch, Punishment, Ice Shard

Sneasel keeps its sharp, hooklike claws retracted inside its paws most of the time. When it's attacked, the claws spring out and rip at the aggressor.

TYPE:
DARK-ICE

Sneasel   Weavile

SNOVER
Frost Tree Pokémon

TYPE:
GRASS-ICE

How to say it: SNOW-vur

Height: 3' 03"
Weight: 111.3 lbs.

Possible Moves: Powder Snow, Leer, Razor Leaf, Icy Wind, Grass Whistle, Swagger, Mist, Ice Shard, Ingrain, Wood Hammer, Blizzard, Sheer Cold

Snover live high in the mountains most of the year, but in the winter, they migrate to lower elevations.

Snover   Abomasnow   Mega Abomasnow

SPEAROW
Tiny Bird Pokémon

How to say it: SPEAR-oh

Height: 1' 00"
Weight: 4.4 lbs.

TYPE:
NORMAL-FLYING

Possible Moves: Peck, Growl, Leer, Fury Attack, Pursuit, Aerial Ace, Mirror Move, Agility, Assurance, Roost, Drill Peck

With its short wings, Spearow has to flap very quickly to stay in the air. It often looks for food hiding in the grass.

Spearow   Fearow

SPINARAK
String Spit Pokémon

How to say it: SPIN-uh-rack

Height: 1' 08"
Weight: 18.7 lbs.

Possible Moves: Poison Sting, String Shot, Scary Face, Constrict, Leech Life, Night Shade, Shadow Sneak, Fury Swipes, Sucker Punch, Spider Web, Agility, Pin Missile, Psychic, Poison Jab, Cross Poison, Sticky Web

While waiting for prey to blunder into its sturdy web, the amazingly patient Spinarak can sit motionless for days at a time.

Spinarak ➡ Ariados

SPINDA
Spot Panda Pokémon

TYPE:
NORMAL

How to say it: SPIN-dah

Height: 3' 07"   **Weight:** 11.0 lbs.

Possible Moves: Tackle, Uproar, Copycat, Feint Attack, Psybeam, Hypnosis, Dizzy Punch, Sucker Punch, Teeter Dance, Psych Up, Double-Edge, Flail, Thrash

Every Spinda's spot pattern is unique. They totter about in a haphazard fashion, which makes aiming at them very difficult.

Does not evolve

STUNFISK
Trap Pokémon

How to say it: STUN-fisk

Height: 2' 04"   **Weight:** 24.3 lbs.

Possible Moves: Fissure, Flail, Tackle, Water Gun, Mud-Slap, Mud Sport, Bide, Thunder Shock, Mud Shot, Camouflage, Mud Bomb, Discharge, Endure, Bounce, Muddy Water, Thunderbolt, Revenge

Stunfisk buries its flat body in mud, so it's hard to see and often gets stepped on. When that happens, its thick skin keeps it from being hurt, and Stunfisk zaps the offender with a cheery smile.

TYPE:
GROUND-ELECTRIC

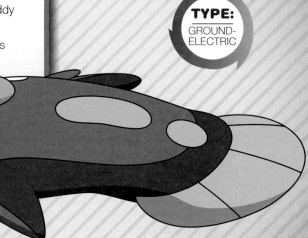

Does not evolve

SUDOWOODO
Imitation Pokémon

How to say it: SOO-doe-WOO-doe

Height: 3' 11"   **Weight:** 83.8 lbs.

Possible Moves: Wood Hammer, Copycat, Flail, Low Kick, Rock Throw, Mimic, Slam, Feint Attack, Rock Tomb, Block, Rock Slide, Counter, Sucker Punch, Double-Edge, Stone Edge, Hammer Arm

For protection, Sudowoodo disguises itself as a tree, though its body seems to be more like a rock than like a plant. It dislikes water and will avoid rain if at all possible.

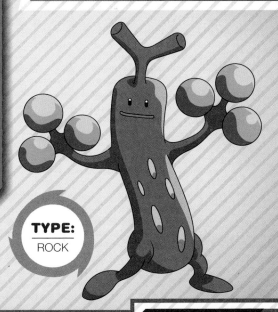

TYPE:
ROCK

Bonsly   Sudowoodo

SWABLU

Cotton Bird Pokémon

How to say it: swah-BLUE

Height: 1' 04"
Weight: 2.6 lbs.

Possible Moves: Peck, Growl, Astonish, Sing, Fury Attack, Safeguard, Mist, Round, Natural Gift, Take Down, Refresh, Mirror Move, Cotton Guard, Dragon Pulse, Perish Song, Moonblast

If a cottony Pokémon flutters out of the sky and lands lightly on your head, it's probably a Swablu pretending to be a hat. No one knows why it does this.

Swablu → Altaria

TYPE: NORMAL-FLYING

SWINUB

Pig Pokémon

TYPE: ICE-GROUND

How to say it: SWY-nub

Height: 1' 04"   **Weight:** 14.3 lbs.

Possible Moves: Tackle, Odor Sleuth, Mud Sport, Powder Snow, Mud-Slap, Endure, Mud Bomb, Icy Wind, Ice Shard, Take Down, Mist, Earthquake, Flail, Blizzard, Amnesia

With its sensitive nose, Swinub can sniff out buried food or the source of a hot spring. If it catches an intriguing scent, it will rush off to track it down.

Swinub   Piloswine   Mamoswine

TEDDIURSA
Little Bear Pokémon

How to say it: TED-dy-UR-sa

Height: 2' 00"　**Weight:** 19.4 lbs.

Possible Moves: Fling, Covet, Scratch, Baby-Doll Eyes, Lick, Fake Tears, Fury Swipes, Feint Attack, Sweet Scent, Play Nice, Slash, Charm, Rest, Snore, Thrash

Teddiursa hides food all over to prepare for the scarcity of winter. Its paws are soaked in honey, so it always has a snack.

TYPE: NORMAL

Teddiursa　Ursaring

TIMBURR
Muscular Pokémon

TYPE: FIGHTING

How to say it: TIM-bur

Height: 2' 00"　**Weight:** 27.6 lbs.

Possible Moves: Pound, Leer, Focus Energy, Bide, Low Kick, Rock Throw, Wake-Up Slap, Chip Away, Bulk Up, Rock Slide, Dynamic Punch, Scary Face, Hammer Arm, Stone Edge, Focus Punch, Superpower

Timburr always carries a wooden beam, which it trades for bigger ones as it grows. These Pokémon can be a big help to construction workers.

Timburr　Gurdurr　Conkeldurr

TORKOAL
Coal Pokémon

TYPE: FIRE

How to say it: TOR-coal

Height: 1' 08"
Weight: 177.2 lbs.

Possible Moves: Inferno, Heat Wave, Protect, Flail, Shell Smash, Ember, Smog, Withdraw, Curse, Fire Spin, Smokescreen, Flame Wheel, Rapid Spin, Flamethrower, Body Slam, Protect, Lava Plume, Iron Defense, Amnesia

Torkoal often take up residence in abandoned coal mines. When threatened, they spew a cloud of black soot.

Does not evolve

TRAPINCH
Ant Pit Pokémon

How to say it: TRAP-inch

Height: 2' 04"   **Weight:** 33.1 lbs.

Possible Moves: Fissure, Superpower, Feint, Bite, Sand Attack, Feint Attack, Sand Tomb, Mud-Slap, Bide, Bulldoze, Rock Slide, Dig, Crunch, Earth Power, Sandstorm, Hyper Beam, Earthquake

Trapinch dig cone-shaped pits in the sand of their desert home. When something falls into the pit, they attack.

TYPE: GROUND

Trapinch → Vibrava → Flygon

TREVENANT

Elder Tree Pokémon

How to say it: TREV-uh-nunt

Height: 4' 11"
Weight: 156.5 lbs.

Possible Moves: Horn Leech, Tackle, Confuse Ray, Astonish, Growth, Ingrain, Feint Attack, Leech Seed, Curse, Will-O-Wisp, Forest's Curse, Destiny Bond, Phantom Force, Wood Hammer, Shadow Claw

TYPE:
GHOST-GRASS

Using its roots, Trevenant can control the trees around it to protect its forest home. Smaller Pokémon sometimes live in its hollow body.

Phantump ➡ **Trevenant**

TRUBBISH

Trash Bag Pokémon

How to say it: TRUB-bish

Height: 2' 00"   **Weight:** 68.3 lbs.

Possible Moves: Pound, Poison Gas, Recycle, Toxic Spikes, Acid Spray, Double Slap, Sludge, Stockpile, Swallow, Take Down, Sludge Bomb, Clear Smog, Toxic, Amnesia, Belch, Gunk Shot, Explosion

TYPE:
POISON

Trubbish live in grungy, germy, grimy places and release a gas that induces sleep in anyone who breathes it. They were created when household garbage reacted with chemical waste.

Trubbish ➡ **Garbodor**

TYRANITAR

Armor Pokémon

How to say it: tie-RAN-uh-tar

Height: 6' 07"
Weight: 445.3 lbs

Possible Moves: Thunder Fang, Ice Fang, Fire Fang, Bite, Leer, Sandstorm, Screech, Chip Away, Rock Slide, Scary Face, Thrash, Dark Pulse, Payback, Crunch, Earthquake, Stone Edge, Hyper Beam, Giga Impact

When Tyranitar goes on a rampage, it causes so much damage to the landscape that maps have to be updated.

MEGA TYRANITAR

Armor Pokémon

Height: 8' 02"
Weight: 562.2 lbs.

TYPE:
ROCK-
DARK

Larvitar   Pupitar   Tyranitar   Mega Tyranitar

URSARING
Hibernator Pokémon

How to say it: UR-sa-ring

Height: 5' 11"
Weight: 277.3 lbs.

Possible Moves: Hammer Arm, Covet, Scratch, Leer, Lick, Fake Tears, Fury Swipes, Feint Attack, Sweet Scent, Play Nice, Slash, Scary Face, Rest, Snore, Thrash

Despite its size, Ursaring can climb to the very tops of trees to find food and a safe place to sleep. It can also sniff out tasty roots buried deep in the ground.

TYPE:
NORMAL

Teddiursa   Ursaring

VANILLISH
Icy Snow Pokémon

How to say it: vuh-NIHL-lish

Height: 3' 07"   **Weight:** 90.4 lbs.

Possible Moves: Icicle Spear, Harden, Astonish, Uproar, Icy Wind, Mist, Avalanche, Taunt, Mirror Shot, Acid Armor, Ice Beam, Hail, Mirror Coat, Blizzard, Sheer Cold

Vanillish live in snow-covered mountains and battle using particles of ice they create by chilling the air around them.

TYPE:
ICE

Vanillite   Vanillish   Vanilluxe

VANILLITE

Fresh Snow Pokémon

TYPE:
ICE

How to say it: vuh-NIHL-lyte

Height: 1' 04"   **Weight:** 12.6 lbs.

Possible Moves: Icicle Spear, Harden, Astonish, Uproar, Icy Wind, Mist, Avalanche, Taunt, Mirror Shot, Acid Armor, Ice Beam, Hail, Mirror Coat, Blizzard, Sheer Cold

When the sun rose and cast its light on icicles, Vanillite were created. With their icy breath, they can surround themselves with snow showers.

Vanillite → Vanillish → Vanilluxe

VANILLUXE

Snowstorm Pokémon

How to say it: vuh-NIHL-lux

Height: 4' 03"   **Weight:** 126.8 lbs.

Possible Moves: Sheer Cold, Freeze-Dry, Weather Ball, Icicle Spear, Harden, Astonish, Uproar, Icy Wind, Mist, Avalanche, Taunt, Mirror Shot, Acid Armor, Ice Beam, Hail, Mirror Coat, Blizzard

TYPE:
ICE

From the water it gulps down, Vanilluxe creates snowy stormclouds inside its body. When it becomes angry, it uses those clouds to form a raging blizzard.

Vanillite → Vanillish → Vanilluxe

VIBRAVA

Vibration Pokémon

TYPE:
GROUND-DRAGON

How to say it: VY-BRAH-va

Height: 3' 07"
Weight: 33.7 lbs.

Possible Moves: Sonic Boom, Sand Attack, Feint Attack, Sand Tomb, Mud-Slap, Bide, Bulldoze, Rock Slide, Supersonic, Screech, Dragon Breath, Earth Power, Sandstorm, Hyper Beam

Vibrava produces ultrasonic waves by rubbing its wings together in a rapid motion. These waves can cause an intense headache.

Trapinch → Vibrava → Flygon

VICTREEBEL

Flycatcher Pokémon

How to say it: VICK-tree-bell

Height: 5' 07"
Weight: 34.2 lbs.

Possible Moves: Stockpile, Swallow, Spit Up, Vine Whip, Sleep Powder, Sweet Scent, Razor Leaf, Leaf Tornado, Leaf Storm, Leaf Blade

Explorers have gone in search of the large colonies of Victreebel rumored to exist deep in the jungle, but they disappeared without a trace.

TYPE:
GRASS-POISON

Bellsprout → Weepinbell → Victreebel

VOLTORB
Ball Pokémon

TYPE: ELECTRIC

How to say it: VOLT-orb

Height: 1' 08"
Weight: 22.9 lbs.

Possible Moves: Charge, Tackle, Sonic Boom, Eerie Impulse, Spark, Rollout, Screech, Charge Beam, Light Screen, Electro Ball, Self-Destruct, Swift, Magnet Rise, Gyro Ball, Explosion, Mirror Coat

Voltorb closely resembles a Poké Ball and often lurks around power plants. People who try to pick it up get zapped.

Voltorb   Electrode

WATCHOG
Lookout Pokémon

How to say it: WAH-chawg

Height: 3' 07" **Weight:** 59.5 lbs.

Possible Moves: Rototiller, Tackle, Leer, Bite, Low Kick, Bide, Detect, Sand Attack, Crunch, Hypnosis, Confuse Ray, Super Fang, After You, Psych Up, Hyper Fang, Mean Look, Baton Pass, Slam

Watchog can make its stripes and eyes glow in the dark. Its tail stands straight up to alert others when it spots an intruder.

TYPE: NORMAL

Patrat   Watchog

WEAVILE
Sharp Claw Pokémon

How to say it: WEE-vile

Height: 3' 07"   **Weight:** 75.0 lbs.

Possible Moves: Embargo, Revenge, Assurance, Scratch, Leer, Taunt, Quick Attack, Feint Attack, Icy Wind, Fury Swipes, Nasty Plot, Metal Claw, Hone Claws, Fling, Screech, Night Slash, Snatch, Punishment, Dark Pulse

In the snowy places where they live, Weavile communicate with others in the area by leaving carvings in tree trunks. They work together to hunt for food.

TYPE: DARK-ICE

Sneasel   Weavile

WEEPINBELL
Flycatcher Pokémon

How to say it: WEE-pin-bell

Height: 3' 03"
Weight: 14.1 lbs.

Possible Moves: Vine Whip, Growth, Wrap, Sleep Powder, Poison Powder, Stun Spore, Acid, Knock Off, Sweet Scent, Gastro Acid, Razor Leaf, Slam, Wring Out

With its sharp-edged leaves, Weepinbell slashes at its opponents. The fluid it spits is extremely acidic.

TYPE: GRASS-POISON

ellsprout   Weepinbell   Victreebel

WHISCASH
Whiskers Pokémon

How to say it: WISS-cash

Height: 2' 11"
Weight: 52.0 lbs.

Possible Moves: Zen Headbutt, Tickle, Mud-Slap, Mud Sport, Water Sport, Water Gun, Mud Bomb, Amnesia, Water Pulse, Magnitude, Rest, Snore, Aqua Tail, Earthquake, Future Sight, Fissure

Whiscash lives at the bottom of a swamp and claims the entire swamp as its territory. It thrashes wildly to startle approaching enemies.

TYPE: WATER-GROUND

Barboach ➡ Whiscash

WIGGLYTUFF
Balloon Pokémon

TYPE: NORMAL-FAIRY

How to say it: WIG-lee-tuff

Height: 3' 03"   **Weight:** 26.5 lbs.

Possible Moves: Double-Edge, Play Rough, Sing, Disable, Defense Curl, Double Slap

An angry Wigglytuff may look much larger than normal, because it will suck in air to puff itself up. Their fur is incredibly soft and snuggly.

Igglybuff ➡ Jigglypuff ➡ Wigglytuff

TYPE:
WATER-
GROUND

How to say it: WOOP-pur

Height: 1' 04"   **Weight:** 18.7 lbs.

Possible Moves: Water Gun, Tail Whip, Mud Sport, Mud Shot, Slam, Mud Bomb, Amnesia, Yawn, Earthquake, Rain Dance, Mist, Haze, Muddy Water

When the sun is out, Wooper stay in the water to keep cool. They go ashore at night, after the temperature drops, to look for food.

Wooper   Quagsire

XERNEAS
Life Pokémon

TYPE: FAIRY

How to say it: ZURR-nee-us

Height: 9' 10"   **Weight:** 474.0 lbs.

Possible Moves: Heal Pulse, Aromatherapy, Ingrain, Take Down, Light Screen, Aurora Beam, Gravity, Geomancy, Moonblast, Megahorn, Night Slash, Horn Leech, Psych Up, Misty Terrain, Nature Power, Close Combat, Giga Impact, Outrage

Xerneas's horns shine in all the colors of the rainbow. It is said that this Legendary Pokémon can share the gift of endless life.

Does not evolve

YVELTAL
Destruction Pokémon

TYPE:
DARK-
FLYING

How to say it: ee-VELL-tall

Height: 19' 00" **Weight:** 447.5 lbs.

Possible Moves: Hurricane, Razor Wind, Taunt, Roost, Double Team, Air Slash, Snarl, Oblivion Wing, Disable, Dark Pulse, Foul Play, Phantom Force, Psychic, Dragon Rush, Focus Blast, Sucker Punch, Hyper Beam, Sky Attack

When Yveltal spreads its dark wings, its feathers give off a red glow. It is said that this Legendary Pokémon can absorb the life energy of others.

Does not evolve

ZOROARK
Illusion Fox Pokémon

TYPE: DARK

How to say it: ZORE-oh-ark

Height: 5' 03"   **Weight:** 178.8 lbs.

Possible Moves: Night Daze, Imprison, U-turn, Scratch, Leer, Pursuit, Hone Claws, Fury Swipes, Feint Attack, Scary Face, Taunt, Foul Play, Night Slash, Torment, Agility, Embargo, Punishment, Nasty Plot

Masters of deception, Zoroark are able to create entire landscapes out of illusions. In this way, they can scare or trick people away from their territory and protect their pack.

Zorua ➡ Zoroark

ZORUA
Tricky Fox Pokémon

TYPE: DARK

How to say it: ZORE-oo-ah

Height: 2' 04"   **Weight:** 27.6 lbs.

Possible Moves: Scratch, Leer, Pursuit, Fake Tears, Fury Swipes, Feint Attack, Scary Face, Taunt, Foul Play, Torment, Agility, Embargo, Punishment, Nasty Plot, Imprison, Night Daze

Zorua can use the power of illusion to make itself look like a person or a different Pokémon. It sometimes uses the resulting confusion to flee from a battle.

Zorua ➡ Zoroark

ZWEILOUS
Hostile Pokémon

TYPE: DARK-DRAGON

How to say it: ZVY-lus

Height: 4' 07"
Weight: 110.2 lbs.

Possible Moves: Double Hit, Dragon Rage, Focus Energy, Bite, Headbutt, Dragon Breath, Roar, Crunch, Slam, Dragon Pulse, Work Up, Dragon Rush, Body Slam, Scary Face, Hyper Voice, Outrage

Zweilous has a ravenous appetite and exhausts the local food supply before moving on. Rather than working together, its two heads compete for food.

Deino → Zweilous → Hydreigon

ZYGARDE
Order Pokémon

LEGENDARY POKÉMON

TYPE: DRAGON-GROUND

How to say it: ZY-gard

Height: 16' 05"
Weight: 672.4 lbs.

Possible Moves: Glare, Bulldoze, Dragon Breath, Bite, Safeguard, Dig, Bind, Land's Wrath, Sandstorm, Haze, Crunch, Earthquake, Camouflage, Dragon Pulse, Dragon Dance, Coil, Extreme Speed, Outrage

Zygarde dwells deep within a cave in the Kalos region. It is said that this Legendary Pokémon is a guardian of the ecosystem.

Does not evolve

Meet the Heroes, Villains, and Professors

ASH KETCHUM

Ash is a ten-year-old boy from Pallet Town in the Kanto region. He's focused on his goal of becoming a Pokémon Master. Since he began his Pokémon journey, Ash has traveled through the regions of Kanto, Johto, Hoenn, Sinnoh, Unova, and now Kalos. His loyal Pikachu is always by his side.

PIKACHU

Ash's constant companion and best friend, Pikachu, is an Electric-type Pokémon. Pikachu has been with Ash since his first days as a Trainer.

Ash is traveling through Kalos with some new friends. Meet . . .

CLEMONT

Clemont is the Lumiose City Gym Leader. He's also a scientist and inventor, though his inventions don't always work the way he expects. His partner Pokémon is Chespin.

BONNIE

Bonnie is Clemont's little sister. She's not old enough to be a Trainer yet, but she loves taking care of Clemont's Pokémon.

SERENA

Serena is just starting her journey in the Kalos region with her first Pokémon partner, Fennekin.

And there's also Kalos's Pokémon professor . . .

PROFESSOR SYCAMORE

The Pokémon professor for the Kalos region, Professor Sycamore's duties include giving new Kalos region Trainers their first Pokémon.

TEAM ROCKET

Since the moment Ash began his Pokémon journey, Jessie, James, and Meowth—also known as Team Rocket—have been one step behind him. They're determined to get their hands on Pikachu. Team Rocket is a criminal organization bent on world domination. Fortunately for our heroes, they're not very good at it.

JAMES

Though he comes from a wealthy family, James chose a life of crime with Team Rocket. He has a soft spot for his Pokémon.

JESSIE

Short-tempered and somewhat vain, Jessie often bosses around her Team Rocket partners. James and Meowth are her closest friends.

MEOWTH

Team Rocket's Meowth taught himself how to speak like a human. He helps Jessie and James with all their criminal schemes.